Here Come the Brides

**An exciting trilogy about triplet sisters
separated at birth—and reunited by love!**

MILLIONAIRE TAKES A BRIDE by Pamela Toth
Special Edition #1353 On sale October 2000

When charming rogue Ryan Noble set his mind
on taking a bride, he did just that. Trouble was, he
claimed Sarah Daniels...the wrong triplet! To make
matters worse, his *un*intended bride's irresistible allure
was stealing *his* heart.

THE BRIDAL QUEST by Jennifer Mikels
Special Edition #1360 On sale November 2000

Runaway heiress Jessica Walker went into
hiding as a nanny for handsome Sam Dawson's
darling daughters. But could the sheriff's
little matchmakers convince Jessica that their
daddy was the husband she'd always longed for?

EXPECTANT BRIDE-TO-BE by Nikki Benjamin
Special Edition #1368 On sale December 2000

Pregnant and alone after an unexpected night
of passion with Jack Randall, her childhood
sweetheart, Abby_____
to single-motheri_____
wanted to make _____ke
no for an answer_____

D0830621

Dear Reader,

As the air begins to chill outside, curl up under a warm blanket with a mug of hot chocolate and these six fabulous Special Edition novels....

First up is bestselling author Lindsay McKenna's *A Man Alone,* part of her compelling and highly emotional MORGAN'S MERCENARIES: MAVERICK HEARTS series. Meet Captain Thane Hamilton, a wounded Marine who'd closed off his heart long ago, and Paige Black, a woman whose tender loving care may be just what the doctor ordered.

Two new miniseries are launching this month and you're not going to want to miss either one! Look for *The Rancher Next Door,* the first of rising star Susan Mallery's brand-new miniseries, LONE STAR CANYON. Not even a long-standing family feud can prevent love from happening! Also, veteran author Penny Richards pens a juicy and scandalous love story with *Sophie's Scandal,* the first of her wonderful new trilogy—RUMOR HAS IT... that two high school sweethearts are about to recapture the love they once shared....

Next, Jennifer Mikels delivers a wonderfully heartwarming romance between a runaway heiress and a local sheriff with *The Bridal Quest,* the second book in the HERE COME THE BRIDES series. And Diana Whitney brings back her popular STORK EXPRESS series. Could a *Baby of Convenience* be just the thing to bring two unlikely people together?

And last, but not least, please welcome newcomer Tori Carrington to the line. *Just Eight Months Old...* and she'd stolen the hearts of two independent bounty hunters—who just might make the perfect family!

Enjoy these delightful tales, and come back next month for more emotional stories about life, love and family!

Best,
Karen Taylor Richman
Senior Editor

Please address questions and book requests to:
Silhouette Reader Service
U.S.: 3010 Walden Ave., P.O. Box 1325, Buffalo, NY 14269
Canadian: P.O. Box 609, Fort Erie, Ont. L2A 5X3

The Bridal Quest

JENNIFER MIKELS

Silhouette®

SPECIAL EDITION™

Published by Silhouette Books

America's Publisher of Contemporary Romance

Special thanks and acknowledgment are given to Jennifer Mikels for her contribution to the Here Come the Brides series.

 SILHOUETTE BOOKS

ISBN 0-373-24360-X

THE BRIDAL QUEST

Visit Silhouette at www.eHarlequin.com

Printed in U.S.A.

Books by Jennifer Mikels

JENNIFER MIKELS

is from Chicago, Illinois, but now resides in Phoenix, Arizona, with her husband, two sons and a shepherd-collie. She enjoys reading, sports, antiques, yard sales and long walks. Though she's done technical writing in public relations, she loves writing romances and happy endings.

You are cordially invited
to the double wedding of

~~Jessica Scott~~ *Walker*

&

Sam Dawson

AND

Sarah Daniels

&

Ryan Noble

Reception hosted by Stuart Walker
at the Walker mansion,
Willow Springs, Nevada

Chapter One

"Lady, what are you doing there?"

Jessica Walker spun around and away from the handwritten Help Wanted sign she'd been reading. Standing in the shadowed light of the moon, she shrank against the window of the local diner behind her. Her heart pounding, she fought panic, and peered at the man approaching her from his car. If only she could see his face.

Darkness shadowed the stairs, but while he climbed them, she gathered an impression. He was tall and broad-shouldered, not old, maybe in his thirties. She saw no more. A beam of light flashed in her eyes, blinding her. She squinted, then looked away from the flashlight he held. "Who are you?" she demanded back to veil fear. It skittered up her spine as he took another step closer.

"The sheriff. Sam Dawson."

Almost on top of her, he lowered the flashlight. She stared hard, saw it now, the badge pinned to a pale, maybe khaki-colored shirt. He was the last person she wanted to see.

"Why don't you tell me what you're doing out here."

She drew a shaky, but calmer breath. She got an image of a good-looking man. Great-looking, she realized when he stepped into the faint light from the diner's sign. He had a face of angles, from the sharp cheekbones and the bridge of the long, straight nose to the strongly defined jaw. Briefly her eyes stopped on his lips, on the full bottom one. "I saw the Help Wanted sign on the window when the bus drove by the diner," she finally answered.

"You came by bus?"

"Yes." She'd thought Thunder Lake, Nevada might be a good place to hide when she'd left her Ferrari in a parking lot blocks from the bus station. Earlier, while riding by, a neon sign for Herb's Diner had caught her eye. By the time she'd gotten off the bus, the diner had closed, and darkness shielded a view of the inside.

"Step over here," he said, urging her out of the shadows and toward the diner's door and the light.

Her heart beat harder as she followed his suggestion and plastered her back to the door.

"Where did you come from?"

Panic rushed her again. What if he asked for identification? "West of here."

"West? That's pretty vague." A thread of annoyance entered his voice. ''West of Thunder Lake? West of Hoover Dam?'' He inclined his head as if trying to see her eyes. ''West of what, mystery lady?''

''I'm not.'' Her fingers tightened on her purse strap.

''Not what?''

''A mystery lady.'' Nerves. She could hear them in the stiffness of her voice.

''What's your name?''

''Scott. Jessica Scott.'' *Oh, please don't ask for identification.* How dumb not to have thought of this problem before she'd taken off. She'd left, deciding to use a maid's last name. She'd reasoned that using Walker, her real name, bordered on idiotic if she didn't want anyone to find her. But her only identification carried the name Walker. She hurried words to steer conversation her way. ''I wanted to read the sign, see if there was a time on the door. I planned to get here early, be the first one applying for the job.''

He sort of laughed. The husky soft sound whispered over her, relaxed her quicker than anything else might have. ''There won't be a crowd rushing the door for the waitress job. Don't worry about it.''

She needed to act normal. Not make him suspicious. ''Oh, that's good.''

''You've been a waitress before?''

She nodded. Liar, liar, pants on fire. She could have told him that she possessed a wealth of other skills. She'd charmed dignitaries during a state dinner at the Governor's house. She'd persuaded a CEO of a major corporation to write a check for her favorite charity.

She'd hobnobbed with high society. But she'd never worked a day in her life.

"Are you visiting someone here?"

Questions. How many questions would he ask? "No." She'd chosen the town on a whim. She'd closed her eyes and had drawn a small imaginary circle on the Nevada map. Her well-manicured fingernail had zeroed in on Thunder Lake. She'd thought it sounded peaceful, envisioned huge pines and a deep blue-colored lake. In retrospect, she believed she should have run to a big city in another state instead of the small northern town in Nevada.

For a long moment, his eyes fixed on her face as if memorizing it. Then he took a more relaxed stance. She assumed he'd decided she wasn't planning to break in. "Where are you staying?"

She had no idea. Uneasiness rushing through her again, she dodged his stare. Several hundred feet away, across the street, a sign for a motel flashed like a welcoming beacon in the night. She spotted the vacancy sign. More important were the words below it. Cheapest rates in town. "Over there," she said, pointing.

A breeze whipped around her, tossing her hair. No longer paralyzed by fear, as the chilly April air sliced through her, she shivered.

"It's cold. You should go to your room. Though this is a small town, it's still not a good idea to be wandering around so late by yourself."

"Late? Nine o'clock is late?" Obviously the streets rolled up early.

She supposed she looked as amazed by his words as she sounded because he offered an explanation. "It is in Thunder Lake. Except in summer when tourists come, it's a quiet town. People work hard here, get up early, go to bed early."

She heard pride in his voice when he talked. Without knowing a thing about Sheriff Sam Dawson, she'd make a guess that he was born and raised here.

"Sounds as if you're used to big-city living."

Instinctively she tensed. Be careful, she warned herself. He was trained to read between lines. "I'll— I should go," she said with a wave of her hand in the direction of the motel. Leaving quickly seemed the smartest thing to do. She gave him a semblance of a smile, hoped it convinced him that she wasn't a fugitive on the run.

"Good night."

She gave up her love affair with the diner door and inched forward. He still hadn't moved. What now? she wondered, nerves jumping as she waited for him to step aside.

"Welcome to Thunder Lake, Jessica Scott."

An almost nervous giggle of relief threatened to slip out. "Thank you." Before she did something dumb and gave herself away, she sidestepped him, then hurried toward the street. She probably wouldn't see him again, didn't have to worry about him.

She passed his car, saw the emblem on the side, signifying Thunder Lake Sheriff's Department. *Great beginnings, Jessica.* Less than half an hour in town, and she'd caught the eye of the local sheriff.

Still feeling edgy, when she reached the street, she dared a look back. He was standing by his car in the shadows. His face was hidden by the darkness, but she just knew he was still watching her.

Chapter Two

For a long moment, Sam stood by a kitchen window and watched a hummingbird hover near a feeder in his next-door neighbor's silver oak. In April, days passed lazily. Before the tourist season of summer, his duties centered on too many meetings with the mayor about requisitions for new cars or uniforms, answering complaint calls and patrolling the town.

He heard chair legs scrape across the kitchen floor behind him, but instead of turning around, he let his mind wander to last night, to the woman he'd seen. About five foot seven and willowy, she'd hardly be a threat to anyone. He hadn't seen her clearly, but she looked out of place standing alone, in the dark, reading a Help Wanted sign. He had questions, but had seen no purpose in keeping her. If she stuck around, got the job, he'd find out more.

As the smell of coffee drifted to him, he turned away from the window. Hinting of the warmer weather to come, bright morning sunlight bathed the kitchen in a warm glow. He moved to the coffee brewer, and began counting drips, waiting for the last one to drop. He needed to quit or cut down, do something. He'd given up smoking long ago, but still needed a quick fix of caffeine to get going in the morning.

"I want to eat the chocolate bears, Daddy."

Grabbing a blue mug from a cup tree first, he swivelled a look over his shoulder at Casey. On a yawn, his youngest plopped on a chair at the kitchen table.

"You should have something more nutrichess for breakfast. Shouldn't she, Daddy?" her older sister piped in. At six, Annie believed in her ability to mother her dolls, her younger sister and sometimes him.

At certain moments, she looked so much like his late wife that his heart twisted. Rail thin, she had shiny brown hair that she'd recently asked to have cut in some trendy bob style. He hadn't resisted. The short cut meant no more mornings struggling with a hair clip or one of those doughnut-looking cloth things, or having to French braid her hair. Now there was a challenge. Give him a perp in an alley any day.

He smiled at the thought. He hadn't encountered one in five years, since he and a pregnant Christina had left Las Vegas, when he'd chosen to be a small-town sheriff instead of another big-city cop.

"Daddy, I want them," Casey insisted, her bottom lip thrusting out.

Back to the chocolate bears.

"There aren't enough left for even one bowl," Annie piped in. "Daddy didn't go to the grocery store yesterday."

Sam cringed at the accusing tone in her voice. She could make that transgression sound like the crime of the century.

Disbelief edged his youngest daughter's voice. "Didn't you, Daddy?" His urchin. With her silky blond hair brushing her shoulders, at four, Casey cared more about making mud pies and riding her new bike with the training wheels than her looks. While her sister had mastered a tone that one day would deliver a reprimand with a few choice words, Sam's youngest needed to say nothing. With one look, she'd drill someone into the ground. He watched her blue eyes narrow. She was a second away from leveling that look at him.

"I bought some," he told her.

Sunshine returned. "You did?" Her face broke into a smile.

Saved by a quick stop at a convenience store last night, Sam mused. "I did."

Annie delivered a pleased grin. "That's good. If there hadn't been more, I would have given you my share," she assured her sister.

Sam closed one eye in her direction. Who was that strange child sitting there? Was this some new phase she was embarking on? He sure had a hard time keeping up. He opened the box of cereal, poured it in two bowls, and set them on the table.

With the girls busy crunching away on the chocolate bears that were swimming in milk and turning it the color of cocoa, he finally poured himself a cup of coffee. He'd bought one of those two-cup coffee brewers for his survival. He never had time to wait for a full pot, and figured there was less waste this way.

"Mrs. Mulvane is here," Casey said with the opening of the back door.

Sam gazed over the rim of the coffee cup at the girls' nanny.

"Good morning." Arlene Mulvane's voice cracked with her bright, cheery greeting. The elderly woman, a grandmother of four, and great-grandmother of two, lumbered into the kitchen. Several months ago after his third nanny had quit, she'd arrived at the door, and said she would take the job. He'd wondered if Arlene and several of the other town do-gooders had drawn straws to see which of them would volunteer to help "the poor dear man alone with those two little girls." Regardless, Arlene had blended in well, treated the girls like her own granddaughters. Though she didn't live in, she would stay late when he couldn't get home on time.

"And we're going to the fire station on our next field trip," Annie was informing Arlene.

Casey offered her opinion. "The lizard farm is better."

"Yuk!" Annie screwed up her nose, but her bright blue eyes shifted to Sam. "Don't forget our date."

He assumed the day would come when some other male would receive that eager look. For now, he had exclusive rights to it. "I won't forget."

"Around twelve-thirty?" Arlene asked.

Sam nodded, then drained the coffee in his cup. On Saturday when they had no school, they met him for lunch. "I'll be at the diner."

The bell above the diner door jingled. Crowded, noisy, the diner, with its blue-and-white decor, held the aroma of perked coffee and freshly baked cinnamon buns. One of the waitresses poured coffee into two thick mugs and plunked them down in front of customers at the counter. Country music from a jukebox played in the background. Another waitress balanced plates along her arm and weaved her way to a booth near the floor-to-ceiling windows.

Jessica had arrived at the diner before dawn broke. Dew had clung to the ground. Now the sun lightened a sky lavish with clouds.

Hurrying toward a customer who'd asked for another glass of water, she was having a terrible morning. Twice, she'd messed up orders. She wondered why she hadn't expected problems. After all, she'd bluffed her way into the waitress job this morning, but she'd truly believed she could handle it. *How foolish, Jessica.*

At the end of the counter, two construction workers from a nearby site waited for a bottle of Tabasco sauce to pour on their eggs, and the fellow in the last booth who she hadn't gotten to yet scowled at the clock on the wall.

"Scott! Your order's up," Herb yelled.

It took a moment to remember to respond to the name. When she'd applied for the job, Herb had questioned why her identification said Walker. She'd claimed she hadn't changed her name back, let him assume Walker was a married name. Briefly she'd held her breath, worried, but busy and distracted, he'd handed her a shirt and had registered no recognition to the Walker name.

Pivoting around, she picked up orders. She abandoned any notion of balancing the plates on her arm. With one in each hand, she started for the table. Better to make several trips than to dump the breakfast on the floor.

"This isn't what I ordered," the man growled when she'd set down his plate.

Sure it was. She was certain she'd gotten the order right. "I'll take care of that, sir."

She placed her reorder, then grabbed the coffee pot to fill cups. At the end of the counter, one customer, a petite woman in her mid-sixties with bright red hair and a broad smile, had been watching her ever since she'd entered the diner. Since all the servers and Herb had stopped to talk to her, Jessica assumed the woman was a regular customer.

"Name's Trudy Holtrum," the woman said. "I heard there was a new waitress."

Jessica paused and filled the woman's coffee cup. "I'm Jessica Scott."

Trudy bobbed her head as if looking for a yes answer to a question not yet asked. "Have you met the sheriff yet?"

Jessica started to frown. Why would she ask such a question? "Yes, why?"

"I work for him," Trudy explained. "Lots of

women in town are willing to give him a run for his money. Are you?''

''Pardon?'' Though stunned by her candor, Jessica laughed.

Hazel eyes met hers with heart-stopping directness. ''Don't you find him attractive?''

Jessica couldn't mask her incredulity. ''What? I don't even know—''

Nothing fazed the woman. ''Better than that, huh?'' She peered over her wire-rimmed glasses at Jessica. ''Handsome? Sexy?''

Politeness stretched only so far, Jessica decided. ''Trudy, I don't think—''

The charms on her bracelet clattered as she set down her coffee cup. ''Oh, he's sexy, all right.'' Grinning, she placed her hands on the counter and heaved herself to a stand.

''See you,'' Jessica said.

''Likely.'' The woman's eyes sparkled. ''Since you and the sheriff might be an item.''

Jessica laughed as Trudy ambled toward the door. The woman was eccentric, probably a gossip and delightful.

As the breakfast rush dwindled down, she refilled water glasses, checked sugar containers and set up several sets of silverware.

By eleven-thirty, the lunch crowd began to wander in. Tables filled quickly. Every stool at the counter was occupied. She noticed that no one sat in her first booth and wondered if she'd already earned a reputation for dropping dishes, and people were avoiding her.

At twelve-thirty, she learned that she had nothing to do with the booth being left empty. She was in the middle of delivering an order of meat loaf when the bell jingled, announcing a customer and she heard Herb's greeting. "Afternoon, Sam. Your usual booth is waiting for you."

The sheriff's usual booth was the empty one in her station.

What happened next really was his fault, she decided. He shouldn't have been so good-looking. Then she wouldn't have been eyeing him instead of watching where she was going. She wouldn't have dropped the tray of dishes.

Plates clattered to the black-and-white tile floor of Herb's Diner. Heads swung in Jessica's direction. And her boss, Herb scowled.

Feeling knots in her shoulders, she rolled them slightly before she began picking up the glass.

A broom in her hand, Cory Winston sidled close to Jessica and began to sweep splintered glass in a pile. "Let me give you a hand." A bottle blond in her early thirties, Cory had worked for Herb since she'd graduated from high school. "Don't feel bad, hon," she said low. "Every single female in town notices him."

Jessica raised a hand and nudged back a few strands of her auburn hair. *Him,* she assumed, was the sheriff.

"But don't get your hopes up. He's a widower, and not looking."

"Oh, that wasn't—"

Cory pushed to a stand before Jessica could explain

that she wasn't interested. Better for Cory to think she was as attracted to the sheriff as every other female. She couldn't have explained that she'd been like a runaway bride. What would she say? *I'm on the run. Hiding from my family. Don't tell the sheriff.* As much as Jessica liked Cory, she couldn't trust her with that secret. "I feel as if I'm on his wanted list," she said, aware of his unwavering stare on her.

Cory laughed, but a speculative tone colored her voice. "He is giving you a lot of attention."

Too much, Jessica thought. She frowned at the broken plate on the floor before her. She would rouse his suspicions if she didn't stop acting so nervous.

There was no real reason for it. Neither her mother nor her grandfather would have notified Willow Springs or any other Nevada police or sheriff departments that she was missing. Her mother's grand sense of propriety demanded a more discreet method for finding her daughter, like a private investigator.

While Jessica gathered the last of the large pieces of broken plates and cups, the diner's dishwasher mopped up the slivers of glass. Jessica thanked him, then hurried behind the counter. Nearby Herb glared. How much would he deduct from her pay for that accident? She needed every penny. For someone who'd never worried about money before, she'd become obsessed with the lack of it lately.

Plastering a smile to her face, she scribbled a customer's order for blueberry pancakes on a ticket. He was a local delivery man, and he'd flirted earlier with her until Cory had commented about his wife and baby girl. Now he halfheartedly smiled, then buried his face in his newspaper. She wished another man would follow suit and not give her so much attention.

Sam considered it part of his job as sheriff to learn about anyone new in town.

Any stranger would have aroused his curiosity. That sounded like a reasonable excuse for keeping an eye on the new waitress at Herb's Diner as she scurried from the cook's station with several plates of pancakes.

But Sam rarely lied to himself. His curiosity about a stranger only partially accounted for his interest in her. True, she looked out of place. Too classy-looking even in the brand-new jeans, snow-white sneakers, and the diner's only concession to a uniform, a blue polo shirt.

She was a leggy woman with shiny auburn-colored hair caught back at the nape of the neck and held in place by a giant gold clip. She had an oval face, soft blue eyes, a straight nose, and a generous mouth. Plain and simple, the woman was a knockout.

Distracted by male voices raised in disagreement, he observed Morly Wells, sitting at a nearby table. A day didn't pass without an argument about something between the retired postal worker and his best friend, Lloyd Guthrie. Sam listened for a moment to them, then shot a look at the clock on the wall above the counter. The girls were late. He thought about a half-finished quarterly statement on his desk that was due in the mayor's office by the end of the week. He should be thinking about budgets and requisitions.

He would have been, but he looked up from the

menu and saw Jessica Scott smile. Not at him, but an old-timer at the counter. Something slow moved through him. He was surprised by it though he shouldn't have been. He'd always been a sucker for a sunshiny smile. But a long time had passed since a woman had really captured his interest. Not since a year and a half ago—when his wife had died.

The clatter of silverware on the floor made him look again in the direction of Herb's new server. The woman had her problems. He saw her picking up the cutlery she'd dropped. While she walked with finishing school grace, she bordered on klutzy. She stopped before Morly to fill his coffee cup, and knocked over a glass of water. Morly jumped back before he wore it. She won't last a week, Sam decided.

Crouching, Jessica gathered the silverware and dumped it on a tray. As she expected, she received the dishwasher's glare. When had she gotten so clumsy, she wondered?

On a sigh, she turned around. Unable to put off the inevitable, she drew a deep breath and headed toward the first booth in her station, toward Sam Dawson.

"I see you got the job."

"Uh-huh," she murmured. Close up, Thunder Lake's sheriff was something, with his sun-streaked brown hair. Faint lines crinkled from the corners of the bluest eyes she'd ever seen.

Again that deep, no-nonsense voice floated on the air. "Herb said you were here at daybreak."

So he'd asked Herb about her. Her stomach clenched. "Yes."

"Have you decided to stay?"

"I'm not sure." Tensing, she tightened her grip on the pencil in her hand. She needed to be friendly, she reminded herself. "The people I've met have been really nice."

"We try to be."

Honest to the core about her feelings, she acknowledged the quickening of her pulse had as much to do with a male-female tug as nervousness. He unsettled her. He made her aware. All good reasons to keep her distance. "Would you like coffee?"

"Dying for one. My dispatcher at the office makes it so strong it tastes like motor oil."

Breathe, Jessica, she berated herself. "We have good coffee here." *He knows that, Jessica.* He's a regular at the diner. "Guess you've had plenty of it."

"Yeah, I have." He presented a warm smile, a knock-your-socks-off smile, the kind meant to tingle a woman all the way down to her toes.

"Do you want to order now, too?"

"No, I'm waiting for others."

She noticed he'd glanced at her left hand. For what? A wedding band?

"Have you been a waitress long?"

She lifted the water glass in front of him. "Oh, sure, for ages and ages."

"That's mine."

Jessica stilled. "What?"

"That was my water glass." He looked at it, then up at her and grinned. "But you can have it."

She heard a hint of humor in his voice. Why? What was so funny? Frowning, she looked down. She didn't need to see herself. She felt the warmth of a blush sweep over her face as she stared at the finger she'd stuck inside his glass. Silently she groaned. When she'd reached for the glass, she'd been thinking more about the gaze on her than what she was doing. What a dumb thing to do. "I'm sorry." She shot a look at Herb, then back at him. "I'll get you another glass." She spoke lightly, even flashed a smile, hoped she sounded relaxed. "And your coffee."

The sounds of two men engaged in a friendly dispute about what teams would play in the World Series this year made him look away. She used that moment to escape. She needed to stop acting so jittery. If he knew who she really was, he would have said something, wouldn't he?

"I told you this might not work," Herb said suddenly, falling in step beside her.

Was he already going to fire her? She wouldn't blame him if he did. She'd dropped several orders of ham and eggs earlier that morning, nearly spilled water on a customer's lap, and probably had caused a shortage of silverware during the diner's busiest hour, sending all that had tumbled to the floor back to the dishwasher. "I'll do better," Jessica promised.

She wished the day was over.

She waited until he walked away, then snatched up the Tabasco bottle. On her way to the customer, unwittingly her gaze locked with the sheriff's. Sympathy darkened his blue eyes. He knew just as Herb and anyone else did that she had no experience. Well, she wasn't doing this by choice. She'd been forced into this situation.

Her mother had announced that she'd found her daughter's perfect match in a handsome, dark-haired male named Ryan Noble. Furthermore, Jessica's grandfather had raved about Ryan, his Golden Boy, the company's most promising associate, and Jessica assumed she'd never convince them that their choice wasn't hers.

All her life she'd tried to please her mother and her grandfather, done everything they'd ever asked her to do. When she declared she wouldn't marry Ryan, an argument had ensued.

Her mother had delivered a steely command. "Ryan Noble is your grandfather's choice. So he'll be yours. Now, you need to meet with him, get to know him better, and stop this nonsense."

Jessica had said no more. She hadn't needed to race down the aisle of the church with the long train of her bridal gown trailing her. No wedding plans existed yet, and she'd vowed there'd be none.

She'd left the room, climbed the stairs to her bedroom, and packed a bag. After everyone went to bed, she'd left a note, saying she'd call shortly.

For the first time in her life, Jessica Walker, heiress to the Walker fortune, did more than balk at doing what her family wanted. She'd fled.

With a few dollars and her credit cards in her shoulder bag, she'd expected to be on a mini-vacation. After spending a few weeks away, she would call home. By then, her family would realize she was serious about not marrying Ryan.

But her plan had crumbled swiftly. Within two days of leaving the family mansion, she'd had to stop using credit cards for rooms and gas when she realized the receipts were traceable.

While in another town, she'd learned that money, something she'd never worried about, was no longer available to her. A trip to a local bank revealed her lack of funds. She'd planned to withdraw a sufficient amount of money, so she wouldn't have to use her credit card. She discovered her account was closed. Usually only the IRS could close someone's bank account, but this one had been opened by her mother when Jessica was still a minor, and all it had taken was Deidre Walker's signature to close it.

Jessica realized then how serious her family was about her marriage to Ryan. A stubborn streak she hadn't even been aware she possessed had flared. She wasn't giving in to their demand. Call her a romantic, but she wanted that happily-ever-after marriage with a man she truly loved. So until she believed her family had accepted her decision, she was on her own.

And not doing well, she reluctantly admitted.

Chapter Three

At the ring of the bell above the door, Jessica looked up from pouring the sheriff's coffee. An ample-hipped, gray-haired woman and two fair-haired minxes rushed in. Jessica smiled at the sight of the green baseball cap propped on the head of the little blonde.

"Daddy," the one with soft brown hair yelled.

Both girls raced from the door ahead of the woman.

With the cup in her hand, Jessica scanned the restaurant for the face of a proud-looking papa. In midstride, she stilled as the two flew to the sheriff's side.

Rapid-fire, they rambled at him. "Amanda is always coloring outside the lines," the youngest was saying in a tone meant to indicate that that was the ultimate no-no. Smiling at her, her daddy lifted the cap from his daughter's head and set it on the booth seat beside him.

Jessica couldn't help smiling. The girls were absolutely adorable.

And motherless.

She recalled that Cory had said he was a widower, and she felt a tug on her heart. *You're too sensitive, Jessica,* her mother had often said. Jessica hadn't thought that was such a terrible trait. She'd admit to having a weakness for children and loved being around them. So what was wrong with that?

She looked forward to having her own some day, and their father would be a man she loved, she reminded herself. That's why she was going through all this. So her family realized that she would accept nothing less.

After she delivered the sheriff's coffee and a hot tea for the woman and chocolate milk for the girls, a brief lunch rush kept her busy. When she looked in the sheriff's direction again, she saw that he'd left his booth to talk to a man sitting at the counter.

Jessica turned in an order for a cheeseburger and fries. Unable to resist, she moseyed over to his daughters. She said hi, but the elderly woman seated in the booth across from the girls was the one who snagged her attention. She looked pale, and beads of perspiration popped out on her forehead. "Ma'am, are you all right?"

The woman sent Jessica a weak smile. "I'm fine."

She definitely didn't look fine.

"Mrs. Mulvane, are you sick?" the oldest girl asked with wide eyes.

"I have this terrible heartburn," the woman was saying. She ran a hand down her throat as if she could ease away the discomfort by touch.

Jessica managed to veil her concern behind a sympathetic smile, then did an about-face. In a few strides, she weaved her way to the sheriff. The idea of not interrupting was never an option. She laid a hand on his forearm to get his attention. When he faced her, momentary puzzlement touched his eyes. "Sheriff, I think the lady with your daughters is having a heart attack."

To his credit, he didn't hesitate longer than a second. "Take my girls to another booth," he demanded, already on his way to them.

Only a step behind him, Jessica hustled the girls from their seats while he bent over the woman. She ushered them with their drinks to a booth at the back of the diner, then blocked their view of the action near the door. "What are your names?"

"I'm Annie," the oldest said. "And this is my sister Casey. I'm six. And she's four. Who are you?"

"I'm Jessica."

"Can I call you Jesse?" the younger one asked.

Jesse. She liked the sound of the name. Different life. Different name. Already Cory had shortened her name to Jess. Why not Jesse? "I'd like that," she said to the little one, and worked to keep them preoccupied enough so they didn't see everyone assisting the woman. "Are you ladies here with your husbands?" she asked, directing her question to Annie who bubbled cheerily and nonstop about everything.

With her question, Casey leaned her blond head

close to her sister's darker one and giggled behind her hand.

"We don't have husbands," Annie said. "We've got our daddy." Pride filled her voice. "He's the sheriff. That's an important job."

Slurping on her straw, Casey craned her neck to see around Jessica. "Uh-huh."

Annie went on, "I go to school. My teacher's name is Mrs. Hooper. Next year I get Mrs. Bowcott. I had chicken pox, a mild case, the nurse told my daddy. But I had funny spots all over."

"Polka dots," Casey said and giggled again.

Jessica smiled along with them. They looked so much alike. Though Casey was a blonde and Annie had brown hair with blond streaks, they had similar heart-shaped faces, pouty mouths, pert noses and large blue eyes.

"Our mommy is in heaven," Annie announced.

Looking solemn, Casey nodded her head.

Jessica studied them both for a long moment, saw no painful grief in their eyes, but was at a loss about what to say. Their daddy unknowingly saved her.

With his approach, Casey jumped from the chair and rushed to him. "Is Mrs. Mulvane sick?" she asked while he lifted her up.

Annie offered her opinion. "Daddy, Mrs. Mulvane looked bad."

Casey nodded. "Real bad."

In a reassuring gesture, he ran a large hand over Annie's head. "The doctors will take good care of her." His eyes shifted from her to Jessica. "Thanks for helping."

"You're welcome." Assuming they'd have plenty of questions for him, she scooted out of the booth so he could slide in. "I'm glad I could help." On that note, she hurried away. Being with his children was one thing, spending any time with him undoubtedly would prove as nerve-wracking as before. She returned to the cook's counter, expecting Herb's censure for sitting so long with them, but he said nothing.

"What you did was nice," Cory whispered when standing beside her and waiting for orders. "In a small town, people help each other without being asked. You aren't as much of a newcomer now."

Jessica warmed. Though she doubted that even her new status would help her keep her job, she learned she'd scored a few points with Herb.

And with two little girls. Before they left, they raced to her with thank-yous that had her smiling most of the afternoon.

A reality check hit at three o'clock. Ready to leave, she stood in the employee break room, thinking about where she could go for the night. She didn't even have a car to sleep in.

She counted her tips and closed her eyes. Her net worth was twenty-one dollars and thirty-five cents. So now what? Before leaving the motel this morning, she'd paid for last night's room with most of her cash. She had no other resources since her bank account was frozen. She'd have to sleep under the stars until she got her paycheck at the end of the week—if she lasted that long.

"You did a good thing with Sam's girls today," a voice said behind her.

She slanted a look over her shoulder at Herb and responded with a smile, truly pleased by his words.

"Want to work extra hours?"

Jessica had learned that the dinner shift belonged to the most experienced waitresses and meant the best tips. He was obviously in a bind or he wouldn't have asked her to stay. Grateful for a chance to earn more money, maybe enough to pay for a motel room tonight, she didn't hesitate. "Yes, I do."

"Okay." That was all he said before leaving her.

A moment later, Cory peeked in. "Chloe didn't show," she said about another waitress. "If you have any questions about the dinner menu, ask me."

By six-thirty the diner was full with dinner customers. So far she'd kept pace with her orders. Well, almost. Herb picked up two customers. Cory, who was working overtime to make extra money for her wedding, took another one. Pleased with how well she'd been doing might have been part of her downfall, Jessica later decided.

Standing in the aisle, she lowered a plate in front of a balding man in a suit. She heard movement behind her and assumed the customer in the next booth was leaving. "Here you are, ma'am," she said to the balding man's companion.

Behind her, a male voice bellowed to someone at the door. "Hey, Marv." At the same moment that Jessica's hand moved down, the man rushed by.

Everything that followed seemed to happen in slow motion. When he hit her elbow, her arm jerked forward. She watched the plate of spaghetti flip out of her hand. The noodles flew from it, plopped onto the table and slid onto the woman's lap.

Jessica moaned.

The woman squeaked.

Unaware, the man who'd bumped her elbow merrily went out the door with his friend Marv.

Feet away, Herb was scowling. Jessica expected his words seconds later. "I'm sorry, I can't afford to keep you," he said, sounding as if he meant that. "But you're a walking disaster. Do you know who's wearing our marinara sauce?"

Jessica shook her head.

"The mayor's wife," Herb told her, and turned away, shaking his head.

Jessica grimaced and headed for the break room to get her suitcase. She saw no point in trying to persuade him to let her stay.

With plates to deliver lining her arm, Cory stepped into her path. "Hon, I'll call you later."

Another problem, Jessica mused. If Cory called the motel, she'd learn she wasn't there anymore. She faced Cory with a brave face, not wanting her to know how devastated she was. "No. I might change motels." Quickly she made a promise. "But I'll keep in touch."

"Okay, but don't worry," she said, closing inches so their shoulders touched. "There are plenty of jobs around town."

Jessica drummed up a smile. She was no more qualified for any other job than she'd been for this one. "Yes, I'm sure there are."

She hadn't thought the situation could get worse.

She'd been wrong. She had no job now, and no place to stay.

Stepping out the back door, she stopped at the wood bench outside Lloyd's Barbershop, the store to the right of the diner. She yanked the clip out of her hair. Hard as she tried, she couldn't squelch the tears. Her throat tightened and her eyes smarted. She'd been so sure she could stand on her own, so sure that once she'd taken this stance against marriage to Ryan Noble that her family would acquiesce. But nothing was going as she planned. Nothing.

Cooking a meal was the last thing on Sam's mind tonight. He didn't mind cooking, but he hated thinking about what to cook night after night. More often than not, he gave in to his daughters' pleas for their favorite food, pizza, so he figured a hamburger at Herb's ranked a close second to a home-cooked meal.

The afternoon had proved long and tense. Not wanting Arlene to be alone, he'd left the girls at the office in the trustworthy hands of Trudy, his assistant and dispatcher, and his girls' great-aunt, then he'd gone to the hospital. While there, he'd contacted Arlene's son in Reno, and a daughter who lived in Fallon, and told them the doctor was keeping their mother in the hospital for observation. He offered reassurances that she was doing fine.

He wasn't.

Sheriff Sam Dawson no longer had a nanny for his daughters. Weary from the events of the day, he wished for a simple answer to his problem, for a way to manage until he found someone to stay with the girls.

A dull headache promised to strengthen if he didn't pop in a few painkillers soon. While he drove with the girls toward the diner for dinner, they'd grown quiet again. He didn't think they were fretting. Earlier, when he'd returned to the office, he'd been met by gloomy faces and their concern for Arlene. Sam had quieted their distress, and worked hard to stir their smiles while they'd settled in the vehicle and fastened seat belts.

Now Annie seemed engrossed in a new book, and Casey was humming to her stuffed dog.

They seemed okay. But what did he know? He was never sure if he was doing the right thing. Being a single dad was tough. He'd never expected to be one, to raise the girls alone. Life without Christina had been difficult, harder than he'd ever imagined. He should have known, expected that. She'd made a difference in his life. She'd come into it when he'd needed someone the most.

She'd been his life, and when she'd died, so had he. For weeks nothing had mattered. He'd been so damn selfish. He'd been thinking only about himself, his pain. Back then, pressure had crowded his throat daily. It was the girls who'd saved him.

They'd given him only a little time to grieve. He'd wanted more. He'd wanted to wallow in self-pity, to let grief crush down on him. But how could he? Life kept intruding. One of them needed new shoes or had a dentist appointment. There were new books to read, a carnival in town, a birthday, Christmas.

His daughters wouldn't let him bury himself in his misery. So he put on a good show. He smiled and laughed because of them. It was his way of telling them everything would be okay, even though it wasn't.

Then during the past months, the terrible ache that had rooted itself within him no longer attacked him with his every breath. Time healed pain. With good intentions, everyone had said that would happen. He hadn't believed them, hadn't believed any woman would reach inside him again, would make him smile. Or love again.

In the rearview mirror, he saw Annie look up from her book. "Isn't she pretty, Daddy?"

He assumed she was talking about some picture in the book.

"And nice," she went on.

"Who?"

"Jesse."

A dimpled smile came to mind. So did shapely legs.

"I like her," Casey announced.

That was a remarkable feat. Casey was stingy with her approvals.

"Do you like her?" she asked.

Like? Maybe. Desire, absolutely. And he wasn't thrilled about that. It was dumb thinking, he berated himself. He hardly knew her.

"I want a hamburger," Annie informed him.

Sam zipped into the parking lot adjacent to the diner.

"Can I have one?"

"Me, too," Casey piped in.

"Sure." He switched off the ignition, watched the girls bound out of their sport utility vehicle. They looked more eager than usual about going into the diner. That made him edgy, especially since Annie's comments about Jessica Scott.

Previously he'd learned from Arlene that his two angels thought they needed a mommy, and their daddy had been too busy to find them one. The truth was he hadn't been looking. He'd had the love of his life. He truly believed a man didn't get that gift twice.

"Daddy, look." Annie pointed in the direction of the bench near Herb's. "There's Jesse."

Sam rounded the front of the vehicle to see them racing toward her and calling her name. "Jesse, Jesse."

He thought she looked tired, but she sat with her back straight as if she was balancing a book on her head. The orange glow of sunset caressed her glossy hair. Hanging loose now, it fell to her shoulders.

From a distance, her smile looked weak. In what seemed like an affectionate gesture, she touched his daughter's shoulder. Closer now, Sam noted the suitcase at her feet, and guessed Thunder Lake's newest resident had a problem. "Hi."

A moment passed before she looked up, swung pale, watery eyes toward him.

Tears. Things had gone from bad to worse for her, Sam deduced. His natural instinct with someone he knew would have been to offer a comforting shoulder. But this woman was a stranger. "Annie, take Casey and go in. Get us a booth."

Nothing was simple with Annie. She liked schedules and predictability. Any deviation from what she expected made her ask a dozen questions. "Aren't you coming?"

"I'll be there in a minute."

A frown grabbed hold on her face. "Where should we sit? What if there aren't any empty tables?"

Here goes, he thought. "Sit in any booth." The parking lot wasn't full, so he doubted they'd have a problem finding one. "And both of you can have a soda tonight," he said, knowing that treat would hurry them into the diner.

They rewarded him with pleased smiles and took off.

Sam focused on her again. "I usually force milk on them," he said lightly to gauge her mood, determine how down she was.

Though she looked tired and worried, a slim smile lit her face.

"I thought you'd want to know what happened with Arlene, Mrs. Mulvane," he said while he sat on the bench beside her. "She got to the hospital in time."

"Oh, I'm so glad."

"The doctor said she'll be fine. Thanks to you. Arlene said she would have never thought she was having a heart attack, she would have written off the pain as heartburn. The doctor said she'd have suffered a lot of heart damage if she hadn't gotten to the hospital when she did. Because of you, she didn't."

"I really didn't do anything. You did." A flush that

made her look younger had swept over her face. "But I'm glad everything worked out for her."

"Me, too. She's a nice woman." As she smiled again, Sam tapped the bottom of her suitcase with the toe of his boot. Not getting involved never entered his mind. This went beyond an obligation to his job. She looked so damn lost, so vulnerable sitting there. "You have a problem?"

In a resigned more than a helpless gesture, she shrugged. "It's nothing."

He didn't believe her for a moment. Whether or not she liked it, he couldn't accept her simple answer. He was used to sticking his nose in others' business. "You had a tough day today. You never waited on tables before, did you?"

A throaty soft laugh answered him. "That's obvious, isn't it?"

Sam stared at her lips and felt an uncharacteristic impatience. "You try hard."

She looked less tense, less annoyed. "That was nice. Thank you."

"But that didn't help, did it?"

She shook her head. "'Fraid not." As a breeze whipped around her and tossed her hair, she raised a hand to brush back strands.

Sam saw no point in beating around the bush. "Did Herb fire you?"

As if sensing it was pointless to pretend she had no problem, she admitted, "Yes, I don't have a job anymore, but I can't blame Herb. I dumped spaghetti on the lap of the mayor's wife."

Despite the seriousness of her personal dilemma, a

laugh tickled Sam's throat. He would have loved to have seen that. Eunice Wilson was big on herself—too big. In her opinion, her husband's political office had made her one of Thunder Lake's most prestigious citizens. "What are you going to do now?"

When her eyes darted to him, he swore he saw panic in them. Hell, he'd been a cop too long. Shyness probably accounted for her quick looks away.

"I'm not sure." Head down, in what he interpreted as a small show of nerves, she fiddled with the strap of her shoulder bag. "Tomorrow I'll look for another job. Cory thought I'd find one without any trouble."

He gave her credit. She hung onto that bright smile as if her life depended on it.

"And if I don't find one here, I'll go somewhere else." She should have stopped then, but she rushed more words. To Sam, it was a sure sign she was nervous, maybe hiding something. "I like to travel, so I move around a lot."

"Jesse. Jesse," Annie yelled as she charged out of the diner and toward them. "Don't you work here anymore?" Looking as if the world's worries rested on her shoulders, she braked a few inches from them.

The smile she gave his daughter was meant to soothe. "No, I don't." Annie swung a distressed look from him to her. Obviously seeing it, too, she offered an excuse to ease away his daughter's concern. "But it's all right. I wanted to look for a different job anyway."

When her hand fluttered to the handle of her suitcase, Sam couldn't help wondering if all that she owned was in it.

"You did!" Delight sparkled in Annie's eyes. "That's good!"

Sam came to attention. What was happening here?

Looking as if she'd burst with joy, Annie bounced in place. "Daddy has a job for you, don't you, Daddy?" There was no stopping her now. In the same breath, she declared, "Daddy's looking for a mommy. He could give you a job."

"A nanny." Sam wondered when he'd lost control of the moment. "What she meant is I need a nanny, not a mommy." Actually, seeing his daughter's cheery, satisfied grin, he wasn't sure what she meant.

Chapter Four

By the flash of humor in Jessica Scott's eyes, Sam guessed he looked as stunned as he felt.

"Thank you, but I couldn't," she said, rescuing him.

Annie's brows pinched together. "But—"

"Annie, we'll ask around for her. See if someone is looking for help." He touched his daughter's shoulder. He would not let a six-year-old maneuver him into a corner. Before the conversation reverted back to her choice for a nanny, he urged her toward the diner. "Come on. We need to join your sister."

"Why can't Jesse be our new nanny?" She repeated that question at least five times during their dinner.

Aware of strength in numbers, Casey joined in. "Why can't she, Daddy?"

"We like her."

"Uh-huh." Casey nibbled on a French fry. "We like her. Don't you?"

"This isn't about liking her." Everyone knew nannies had gray hair and orthopedic shoes. "I don't even think she'd want the job."

Questioningly Casey tipped her head. "Why wouldn't she?"

How innocent they were. Sam ran a finger down her nose to make her giggle. Not everyone thought they were angels like he did. "Drink your soda."

"Who's going to take care of us then?" Annie cut in.

Good question, Sam mused. The whole incident with Arlene could have been worse if Jess hadn't helped. *Jess.* So he thought of her that way. Wasn't that warning enough? He would be asking for trouble if he hired her. Only a dumb man willingly brought a woman into his house who stirred more feeling in him than any woman had in almost two years.

But she really was good with the girls. Oh, hell. He could stifle whatever attraction was simmering for her. More important was getting someone for his daughters.

Despite their certainty that she'd be perfect for them, he needed to know more about her than her name. "I'll be right back." He left them, scoffing down a favorite dessert, chocolate cream pie, and crossed to Herb.

Herb told him that he liked her. That's what everyone said. After he asked Cory a few questions, Sam called the motel owner from Herb's office phone. According to Josie Colten, Jess hadn't charged the room on a credit card. Sam deduced that meant she believed in paying cash for everything, or she'd filed bankruptcy and had no credit. Who knew if she'd suffered hard times?

Herb believed she needed money but she'd refused when Cory had offered her some. Sam figured she was proud. He considered that a good trait. He believed if a person had one good trait they possessed others. He wasn't naive, but he was a fair lawman, one who never judged everything in terms of black or white. To be too rigid was just plain stupid.

Both girls angled expectant looks at him when he returned to the booth.

"I'll ask her," he told them.

"Yippee!" Casey bounced up and down on the booth seat.

"We'll try her." He'd already listed reasons to offer her the job. Besides showing common sense for the girls as well as Arlene, he'd seen a gentleness in her touch with Casey. He considered himself a good judge of character, and felt the girls would be safe with her. They certainly liked her. And she needed the job. "Remember. She might not work out," he reminded his daughters.

"Yes, she will," Annie insisted.

"We'll see."

With no room, no money, and no job, for privacy Jessica strolled to the nearby gas station and the public phone instead of using the phone inside Herb's

Diner. She hated to admit defeat, but she had no choice. She had to call home.

Inside the phone booth, she left the door open and fished in her shoulder bag for coins. How much would she need for a long-distance phone call?

"Jesse, Jesse." She heard the sweet little voices a second before Annie and Casey appeared at the door.

Through the glass, Jessica observed their father's approach.

Casey squeezed into the booth as if needing to get closer. "Jesse, will you be our nanny?"

"Will you, Jesse?" Annie asked, crowding in, too.

Standing behind them now, their father gave her that killer smile again. "Girls, let me talk to her."

Casey whirled around, inched out of the booth behind her sister. Halting beside him, she tugged on his hand, forced him to bend over. "Make her, Daddy," she said in a low whisper.

"I'll do my best," he whispered back. "We're serious," he said when the girls stepped away. "We'd like to offer you the nanny job. It's full-time. Live-in."

Jessica's heart galloped. He was suggesting all she wanted. A job, a place to stay, another chance. "I have no qualifications for the job."

"You like kids."

"I love them, Sheriff."

"Sam," he corrected. "And my girls like you. Look, I'm a widower, so like I said, we need a live-in."

She wanted to search his eyes for grief, but he looked away to check on his daughters. When he looked back, she saw curiosity in his eyes. "You're not married or—"

"I'm not," she cut in before he could finish. Inwardly she tensed. What else would he ask? "But I have worked with children from disadvantaged homes," she said, hoping a little information would keep him from asking questions she didn't want to answer. "It wasn't a job. Volunteer work," she added.

His eyes sharpened, filled with questions, but he steered the conversation down a different path. "Herb said good things about you."

"How could he?" She couldn't help but laugh as she thought of how often she'd goofed. "I nearly broke all of his dishes."

"He said that, but he also said you were honest, never touched others' tips."

Honest. Tension clenched her stomach. "Did he say anything else?" Like her name was really Walker.

"Don't frown. He said nothing bad. He told me you were a good employee. Willing to help. Friendly to everyone."

She blushed. "That was nice of him."

"Those are good reasons to hire someone."

This couldn't be so easy. She glanced toward the girls who were standing by the bench. Would he really hire her based on a few things someone said about her?

"It's been difficult finding a nanny who works well with us," he said suddenly.

Now that made no sense to her. She spoke her thoughts. "Why? Your daughters are adorable."

"I think so. I'm glad you do. I'd prefer to hire someone who sees all of my daughters' fine qualities, and not their faults." The laughter in his voice died with his next words. "But I should explain. We lost the first nanny because Annie was missing her mommy and wanted no substitute of any kind. The next nanny failed to pass Casey's test."

"Her test?"

"Casey's her own person. Some people don't understand that. One nanny called my youngest weird. The one who worked for me before Arlene was annoyed that I came home so late. No explanation mattered. She didn't want to hear one. I'm a sheriff. Sometimes I can't leave. She didn't understand. Do you have a problem with that?"

"No." She wanted to hug him for solving her problems. "But I have to be fair. If I get the job, it would only be temporary. I can't stay for long." She expected questions now, and worried he would consider that a good reason not to hire her. "I want the job," she added on a rush. "I need the job." Slowly he grinned and Jessica saw then why he *really* had a reputation for curling toes. A rush of warmth swept through her.

"And we need you."

How could everything be so wrong one minute and so right the next? she wondered.

He braced a shoulder against the opened folding door. "Want to know anything about me, about us?"

Cory and several other servers had informed her about one of Thunder Lake's most eligible males. He was honest and hardworking, and would do anything for his daughters. He was also considered a real catch by most single women in town. They'd claimed he was fair and compassionate. He was well-liked, well-respected, but could be tough when necessary.

And he was brave, Cory had assured her, then had gone on to tell a story about how he'd single-handedly brought in an escaped convict who'd been hiding in an abandoned farmhouse outside of town. "I already know all about you." She felt a blush sweep over her face. When had she become such a motormouth?

He made no comment about what she'd said, but a smile twitched up the corners of his lips. "Give me an hour to delegate a few jobs to my deputy, then I'll meet you at my house, show you your room and you can settle in." He withdrew a pad of paper from his front shirt pocket, yanked a sheet of paper from it. Using the frame of the phone booth for a writing surface, he scribbled down the address.

Peripherally Jessica saw the girls inching closer.

So had he. He paused in writing. "She said yes."

"She said yes!" Annie repeated.

Displaying typical four-year-old exuberance, Casey jumped up and down. "Yippee!"

"As you can see, they're happy." He handed her the paper with the address. "On their behalf, thank you."

Jessica felt as if she should be saying that. She stepped out of the booth, dropped the coins for the phone call back in her shoulder bag and watched him slip his hand around Casey's.

Over her shoulder, Casey looked back and waved.

Annie gave a look back, too, and sent Jessica one of her hundred-watt smiles.

In that second, she knew that she didn't want to lose this job. She almost felt guilty about getting paid for it. She read the address first, then pocketed the paper.

All seemed perfect, but she'd need different clothes, wouldn't she? She'd never fool him if she wore designer T-shirts and jeans. She crossed the street to browse through a thrift shop. Lucky for her it was open this one evening of the week. Using part of the thirty-three dollars and seventy-five cents that she'd collected in lunch and dinner tips, she purchased several T-shirts and another pair of jeans.

She stuffed the new items into her suitcase, then started walking toward his house. She'd been so thrilled to get a job that nothing else had mattered. She hadn't asked what he would expect her to do. She'd assumed she would watch the girls. Would he want her to do more? Housekeeping? Oh, how difficult could it be to run a vacuum cleaner? Sounds good, she mused. Keep convincing yourself you can handle this. All she'd have to do is learn which buttons to push on the dishwasher and washing machine, how hard could that be?

Three blocks away from the town's business district, she turned down a street of huge pines and silver oaks. Unlike the ranch-style homes near the edge of the town, the sheriff and his daughters lived in a house reminiscent of a 19th-century farmhouse with two French-pane windows upstairs, and four on the first floor. It was painted brownish-red with a white door and white trim around the windows. A cobble-stone walkway led to the three front steps and the front door. Several huge pines shaded the house from the late afternoon sun.

Jessica leaned against the white wood railing to wait. It wasn't long. Within minutes, a vehicle zipped around the corner and pulled onto the driveway.

"Jesse, Jesse," Casey yelled when she opened the vehicle's door. Wearing a baseball cap, khaki pants, a blue-and-white striped top, and sneakers, she bounded toward the house. Jessica smiled at the wallet-sized, red shoulder bag hanging from Casey's shoulder. She'd definitely set her own style.

"We hurried home," Annie informed her, coming in second in the race with Casey. "We'd have been here sooner, but Daddy had to give Humphrey a ride home. He's Mrs. Olsen's dog."

Sam strolled up, shaking his head. "If you let her, she'll tell you about every person in town."

"Daddy says I like to talk." All innocence, Annie grinned up at him. "Don't you, Daddy?"

His knuckles stroked her cheek lovingly. "I hope you haven't been waiting here too long."

"Hardly at all," Jessica assured him.

"Good." Sam stepped up to the door. "Let's go in."

The front door opened to a short foyer and the stair-case to the second floor. To her right was the living room with a comfy-looking sofa in a deep blue color and several chairs in a blue-and-maroon pattern.

"It needs a little picking up." He skirted the coffee table to snatch up the newspaper that was strewn across the sofa cushions, then gestured to his right. "The kitchen is this way."

Jessica nodded and traced his steps through a formal dining room with a highly polished cherrywood table and chairs and a breakfront. A collection of china cups, a crystal decanter and wineglasses occupied the shelves. A few steps behind him, she entered the kitchen to see him plugging in the coffee brewer.

Done in oak, the kitchen was a large, sunny room, the result of French doors that led to the backyard. A round oak table and cane chairs rested on a multicolored braided rug.

"I'll show you your room," Annie volunteered.

"I will," Casey insisted.

Sam ran interference. "You both can."

Together they went upstairs. Feeling a touch uneasy in her new surroundings, Jessica hoped that once she could call someplace home, even temporarily, she'd begin to relax.

Casey's chattering about her favorite cartoon movie, the one about ants, helped. Noticing her small hand's possessive hold on the purse, Jessica assumed it was a treasured item. "I like your purse."

"She carries it everywhere," Annie said from behind them.

A little huffily, Casey raised her chin. "I like it."

Jessica sensed the start of an argument. "Will you show me your rooms first?" she asked to sidetrack them from their dispute.

At the landing, Annie pointed to her left. "My room is that way." Eagerly she steered her toward a feminine room done in purple and white with a white canopy bed and a collection of dolls at center stage on shelves lining one wall.

Casey's room contained the usual four-year-old toys, but it was done in mostly green, and a giant picture of a black-and-yellow butterfly adorned one wall. A baseball mitt and cap were tossed in a corner of oversized pillows, and propped nearby was an oversized stuffed animal, a green ant.

"Do you like mine?" Casey asked.

She chose an answer that would prevent hurt feelings. "I like both of them." A hand on their backs, she urged them into the hallway. Noticing Sam waiting by a door halfway down the hall, she hurried there.

He opened the door for her, and flicked on a wall switch. "Everything was redecorated by Trudy after Christina, my wife, died."

Jessica stepped in. Had he sought change to forget what had been?

"If you knew Trudy, you'd be amazed how well it looks. Everything is so normal-looking."

"I met Trudy," she said, taking in the room. It was homey and clean-looking with a mahogany chest of drawers, and a small, mahogany writing desk. Near the window was a pale wood and hunter-green chair. A print of a Monet adorned the wall above the bed with its white bedskirt and a green, white and pink basket quilt. "She said that she worked for you. Is she the one who makes coffee that tastes like motor oil?"

A laugh clung to his voice. "She's the one."

"She takes a personal interest in you."

Sam groaned and sent her a knowing look. "Did she ask you if your intentions were honorable about me?"

He knew the woman well. "Sort of."

"She figures she has a right since she's family. Christina's aunt."

Jessica matched his smile. "The room is lovely."

"I'm glad you like it." His lips curved in a pleased smile. "After you get settled, come downstairs. I'll give you coffee."

"I'll come now." Jessica trailed him out of the room. "I don't have much to unpack."

On her way to the kitchen, she scanned rooms, noted photographs of the girls, a piano in the corner of the living room, shelves of books, mostly mysteries. The house was cozy, welcoming.

In the kitchen, she spotted a small plant on the kitchen windowsill. School papers held with magnets clung to the refrigerator. "Annie got a gold star," she said about one of the papers.

"She works hard for them." His back to her, he removed two blue mugs from a mug tree. "She's a good student."

"I'd have guessed that."

"Sometimes she's six going on thirty," he said while pouring their coffee. "She has been more affected by all the different nannies than Casey. But like I said, it's hard finding someone. What we need most is someone who'll stick around."

Jessica quickly reminded him, "I explained that I'd only take this job for a little while."

"I know. I appreciate your honesty."

His words made her cringe. She wasn't honest, not at all. And though she wasn't sure how long she'd stay, she knew she couldn't offer the girls the stability he was looking for in their nanny. Actually she had no definite plans and had given her future little thought. She'd hoped her leaving home would make her mother and grandfather believe that she was serious about not marrying Ryan Noble. She'd believed if they really cared about her, then they'd want her happy.

"Want milk or sugar?"

She shook her head. Until she was sure her family understood she meant business, she needed the job. But she realized how unfair that was to Sam and the girls. "I'll try to stay until the end of May. Would that help you?" A month or so was the best she could give him.

"It might." He handed her one of the mugs. "By then, some of the college kids will be home for the summer." Cautiously he sipped his coffee. "Have you had dinner?"

His question sparked one of her own. "Do you want me to cook? Will that be part of my job?"

While she stayed by the table, he braced his backside against the kitchen counter. "I'd hoped—do you cook?"

She loved to, but at home her mother would have been aghast if she spent even a few hours in the kitchen. "Yes. Do you?"

He pulled a face. "Grudgingly. If you haven't eaten, you're welcome to dig in and have whatever you want."

She wandered to the windowsill, stared at the pot of soil and the little sprout. "I'm not really hungry," she answered, but she eyed an apple and a banana in a wicker basket of fruit in the center of the table. "Do I have other duties?"

"What about cleaning and laundry? Will you do them?"

Of course he'd suggest that. She'd told Herb that she'd done "this and that, been a sales clerk, an elderly woman's companion, a maid."

"If you don't want to, it's all right, Jess."

She liked the way he'd said her name—smooth, easy and with a friendliness that bordered on affectionate.

"But—" A wry smile curved his mouth. "It would help me a lot. I can't be a good daddy, a good sheriff and handle those jobs, too." Jessica heard a trace of guilt in his voice, and quickly concluded he wouldn't have felt that if he wasn't so loving, so caring. "I need help. And you're it."

Poor man. He had no idea that he was about to rely on someone who had no idea how to operate a washing machine, a vacuum cleaner or a dishwasher. She wasn't dumb, she had degrees in anthropology and medieval history, but just no practical life experience. "I'll do whatever I can to make things easier for you." She hadn't exactly lied. She would try. That didn't mean she would succeed.

"I'm usually home at the girls' bedtime."

"When is that?"

He grimaced as if uncomfortable with his answer. "When I get home. Schedules aren't set in stone around here. Anyway I don't want to get off on the wrong foot, but I might as well get this out in the open now. I hired one nanny who tried to take over. The girls are mine. I raise them.''

Jessica couldn't find fault with his responsible attitude toward his daughters. ''It seems you've done a great job.''

''Thanks. But I've been permissive while trying to fill the gap left by the absence of their mother, and as you probably noticed, their rooms look like toy stores. When my wife died, the town became our family. Women brought over dinner every night, gifts were given to the girls. Everyone spoiled them—us,'' he said on a laugh. ''Until I said, 'no more.'''

Looking down, he shoved back his shirt cuff and eyed his watch. ''I have to leave. I asked one of my deputies to stay late so I could be here and get you settled in.''

Jessica listened and nodded while he discussed salary and days off.

''Will you be okay?'' he questioned as he lifted the jacket to his uniform from the back of a kitchen chair.

She nodded again. ''Oh, we'll be fine.'' She really believed that. She watched him leave the room, then snagged an apple. What she wanted most was quiet time to enjoy her sudden good luck.

Sam kept thinking about them. Though not worried, he wondered if he was nuts. He was trusting her with his children and he hardly knew her.

All he knew about her, he'd learned from Cory. Thunder Lake's newest resident was twenty-six. Born in Nevada. Where? Cory hadn't known. Somewhere near Reno, she thought. Jess never mentioned family, claimed she had no brothers or sisters.

According to Cory, among the tidbits of information Jess had told her, she jogged every morning. She loved pecan pie. Cory had thought some man had broken her heart. Nothing revealed why she'd come to Thunder Lake. Since she'd told no one, he figured she was low on trust.

But he'd get answers. A patient man, he was willing to wait awhile. When working on the police force in Las Vegas, he'd once kept a file open long after his captain had told him to consider the case unsolved.

He didn't give up on anything easily. He would learn what her story was. In the meantime, he would keep a close eye on her. It was part of his job to look out for the welfare of others.

Jessica truly liked being around children. She might never have realized that if she hadn't volunteered to help with children from disadvantaged homes. Because of her background, she'd thought she would never relate. But she'd found that her love of kids bridged the differences. It wasn't always easy. Often they rebuffed kindness or attention. Jessica developed thick skin. She understood they'd been rejected so many times they lacked trust. But the two little girls she was with now carried none of the same burdens. They were loved.

She spent the first hour asking about their routines, trying to become familiar with schedules, and discovered they had none. Though wake-up was a specific time, their daddy allowed them a lot of leeway about their bedtime.

She assumed he had a hard time playing disciplinarian when they were all still handling grief. At least, he was. Annie had admitted she could hardly remember her mommy except that she'd smelled nice and had sung a song about sunshine to her. When Casey left the room, Annie whispered that Casey was too young to remember any of that. That left Jessica with the conclusion that Sam, not they, still needed healing from the loss.

As the clock neared nine, Jessica urged them to take baths and put on their pajamas. She finished buttoning Casey's pajamas while Annie brushed her hair. "Time to brush teeth."

"We have to floss, too. Daddy won't let us go to bed unless we do," Annie told her between scrubbing the brush across her teeth.

With rituals done, she settled with them in the living room. She perused the television guide for a few minutes, then chose a movie-length cartoon.

In fifteen minutes, Casey gave in and slumped to her left side, using Jessica's lap for a pillow. A night-owl, Annie fought sleep. Head bobbing, she finally dozed off at eleven o'clock and slid down on the sofa cushion.

"They need a bedtime," Jessica muttered.

"I know," a masculine voice said unexpectedly from the doorway.

Her head snapped up. She'd had no warning he was near, had heard no footsteps, no opening and closing of the door. "You are quiet." Embarrassed at being caught talking to herself, she felt heat in her cheeks.

"I practice so I can catch my deputies sleeping."
Sam shrugged out of his jacket and glanced at his
sleeping daughters.

"They didn't make it," Jessica said the obvious as
she eased out from under Casey and off the sofa.
Bending over the table, she scooped up several of
Annie's books to stack them.

"They often don't. I had to stay late. There was a
call at the lake about someone fooling with the boats.
It was a false alarm, one of the owner's grandsons
forgot his sweater in the boat and went back for it."

Straightening, she gave him a sleepy smile.

"You look tired."

So did he. But he also looked more relaxed. "A
little. Annie read a few books to us," she said quietly.
"And we watched the cartoon about the Dalmatians."

"It's a favorite of Annie's," he said equally low
so he wouldn't wake the girls.

Jessica smiled easily. She hoped they'd do this often, meet during the quiet moments to talk after the
girls had gone to sleep. "I'll help you carry them to
bed," she said, moving to Casey.

"You don't have to—"

Jessica already had Casey in her arms.

For a brief second, a look had darted across his
face. She didn't know him well enough to read what
it meant. But she'd felt as if she'd stepped out of
bounds when she'd picked up his daughter. "Is it
okay? If you don't want me to—"

The look passed as quickly as it formed. "It's okay.
Thanks," he said, gathering up Annie.

Jessica cradled Casey's head close to her breast,

then followed him up the steps. Possibly she'd read him wrong.

While he carried Annie into her room, she took Casey into hers. Within seconds, he came in, bent over the bed and kissed his daughter's forehead.

It was such a touching moment. Jessica couldn't recall such a display of tenderness in her family, ever.

She stood near the end of the bed, waited, watched his large hand stroke Casey's forehead, gently brush back a few strands of her pale hair from her cheek. When he turned, she expected him to lead the way out of the room. Instead, he paused near the doorway, stood inches from her, facing her.

In the dim glow of the night light, his eyes, so dark she felt as if she could get lost in them, fixed on her. He stood still, the heat of his breath falling across her lips. "I'm glad you're here, Jess."

Her heart thudded harder. "Thank you." Was she imagining that he'd moved closer? Maybe she had. "So am I."

As she smiled, he seemed to straighten his back, draw away. "Good night."

"Good night." Confused, she stared after him. She was not prone to a wild imagination. And she was not naive or inexperienced. Being close to a man had never fluttered her heart. But unexpected feelings had definitely swarmed in on her just now. And with them, a warning rang in her mind.

She definitely couldn't afford to do anything dumb. What she had to remember most was how much she needed this job.

Chapter Five

Jessica reinforced similar thoughts the next morning while dressing. Involvement with him would only complicate her situation. Whatever she'd felt had happened was because he'd been nice, nothing more.

Yawning, she glanced toward the window. A gray morning sky promised rain. She felt a chill in the air and tugged on jeans and a hunter-green sweatshirt. After a run to the bathroom, she checked the girls' rooms to see if they were awake. Both rooms were empty.

Frowning, she rushed back to her room. She never expected them to be up so early. She wiggled her feet into sneakers, then tackled bed-making. She successfully made a bed for the first time, though it took her several tries to get it to look right.

While descending the steps, she caught a whiff of brewing coffee. Swell. He hired her to do a job, and she slept in. When her foot hit the last step, the sounds of girlish laughter and a masculine chuckle reached her.

"Who said he could eat a whole watermelon?" Sam was asking.

"Garrett. He always tells stories," Annie added.

Over her head, his eyes locked with Jessica's. "Good morning. Sleep well?"

She sniffed the rich aroma of the coffee. "Wonderfully." She wasn't lying. For the first time since she'd left her home, she'd fallen asleep easily, not edgy about every noise she heard.

"We have chocolate bears," Casey informed her between spoons of the cereal. "Do you want some?"

"No, I'll have—" What will you have? She mentally berated herself and clamped her lips shut. *You have no servants.*

Sam looked up from buttering toast. "What?"

"Nothing. I was going to say that I'll have to get up earlier."

"We figured you could sleep in today." He held up the bag of bread. "Want toast?"

"Yes, thank you." Jessica stood to the side, soaking in the smell of the toasting bread, the aroma of coffee, the two little girls jabbering between spoons of cereal, and the handsome male looking so comfortable and at ease in the kitchen.

A disturbing thought nagged at her as the girls turned matching smiles on her. They were all trusting her, welcoming her. Nice as that was, it made her feel even worse about the deception.

"We have grape and strawberry jelly," Sam said.

"I like strawberry best," Casey told her.

"I do, too," Jessica responded. She ambled to the coffeepot and poured a cup. Over the rim of it, she regarded them. Something was said and laughter rang out. Smiling along, she joined them at the table.

Breakfast played out so differently from any meal she'd ever had at home. The girls chattered, milk was spilled, laughter punctuated the air more than once.

When the girls excused themselves, then went off to play, Jessica said what had been on her mind. "I don't understand something. I find your daughters to be wonderful and well-behaved. Why did you really have a nanny problem?"

Looking down, he wiped a napkin between his hands. "I'll let you decide for yourself. One morning all of the glasses were missing. Casey had taken them outside. The nanny of the day wasn't thrilled to find grasshoppers crawling around in each of them."

Jessica couldn't help smiling.

"She likes bugs," he said simply with a shrug. "Most women don't. Another nanny, Lucille—well, she didn't understand the girls—didn't try to." He curled fingers around a blue mug. "She had fits because she'd just come back from the grocery store and the bread was missing. 'The birds were hungry,' Casey had said."

Jessica thought the action was sweet and caring.

Obviously Sam had, also. "She was with us for two days." He moved to the sink and rinsed out his cup. "Has my youngest daughter shown you the inside of her red purse yet?"

"What about it?"

"Look in it. Then you'll know."

Jessica didn't ask more as the girls rushed in, rambling about "a really neat game" that had been advertised on television.

Sam gave them a, "we'll see", for an answer, then bent over and kissed each girl. "I'll be home for dinner."

"Is there anything you want me to do?" Jessica asked.

"No. I'll grill steaks." At the door, he glanced back. "If you need anything, call the office. Even if I'm not in the office, someone will get in touch with me—if you need me."

Jessica answered with a smile. *If she needed him?* She was certain a lot of women in town would admit to needing him.

"I have a secret," Casey whispered suddenly against Jessica's ear, snapping her back.

Obviously Casey planned to tell it. "It's Daddy's birthday," she said just as softly though they were the only two in the room.

Jessica wondered if that was true. "When? Today?"

"No. Later."

Jessica decided to talk to Annie or Trudy and learn specifics. "Are you having a party?"

Her eyes went wide. "Could we?"

Jessica wasn't certain Sam wouldn't mind. "I'm not sure. But I'll find out if that's a good idea."

* * *

Sam closed the heavy double door in the county sheriff's building that separated the cells from the outer room. Simply furnished with old oak desks and straight-back chairs, it had been painted an eye-pleasing beige.

He genuinely liked his two deputies. Gary was a wiry, younger man with reddish hair and a gangly build. Tony was a short, stout man in his late fifties with graying hair and a thick gray mustache. They were congenial, content with the slow pace of their jobs.

This morning's biggest crime was a broken display window at Holden Sporting Goods. Over a decade ago, Sam had left Thunder Lake to attend a police academy. He'd learned police procedures—ballistics, forensics, everything he'd probably never have a use for in the small town. Sometimes he missed the quicker pace, the excitement of a big city, but he reasoned that the sheriff's position gave him more freedom to be a good father.

"Did you take time for breakfast?"

He zeroed in on Trudy. She'd had the job as his right hand from the first day he'd gotten the sheriff's job. She had a penchant for wearing noisy bracelets and changing her hair color. This week her short, boyish cut had been colored to match the red of the new stop sign at the edge of town.

"I did," he answered.

"Heard you have a new nanny," she said out of the blue after he dropped to the chair behind his desk.

Sam wondered who her spy was, then remembered the girls had called her early this morning. "You mean, you didn't check her out when she was working at the diner?''

Trudy cast a crooked grin at him. "Of course, I did. She's a pretty thing. But she wouldn't win a Waitress of the Year award.''

Sam had thought that was obvious.

Papers in hand, Trudy crossed to his desk. "Now that she's working for you, are you going to date her?''

Head bent, Sam skimmed the fax she'd dropped in front of him rather than meet her curious stare. "Never said I was.''

"You need to date.''

"I've dated.''

Trudy snorted. "Going out with Liz doesn't count,'' she said about his neighbor.

"Why doesn't it?''

"Because you've known her since you were ten years old, and you wouldn't be interested in her.''

She was right, of course.

"It'll be two years soon.''

"In another six months,'' he was quick to point out. But who's counting? There was a time after Christina died, he could have ticked off the days, hours, minutes since the doctor had stepped into the emergency waiting room and his and the girls' lives had crashed.

"You need a wife, a soul mate. Christina would want that for you.''

There was truth in Trudy's words. Christina was one of the most generous, caring people he'd ever met. She'd want him happy and loved. She'd want her daughters to have a mommy.

For a long time, he wasn't comfortable with the idea of any woman taking Christina's place in his life or his heart. But he knew they needed what was missing in their lives—the softness of a woman.

"The girls are looking," Trudy said, cutting into his thoughts. "Want their list of candidates?"

Good-naturedly he endured her meddling. He knew as Christina's aunt that her intentions were well-meaning, that she loved him like her own. The problem was she wanted something for him that he wasn't sure he wanted—love.

Sending her a deadly look over his shoulder, he strode toward the door. "I'll pass." Behind him, he heard her cackle before he stepped outside.

He didn't care what woman she or his daughters had come up with. He was having enough trouble with too many thoughts about a certain redhead. An image of Jess holding Casey last night lingered in his mind. He'd never seen Casey in any woman's arms but Christina's or Trudy's. Breath had stuck in his chest. But then Jess had been tying him in knots since the moment he'd first seen her.

Last night he'd tried to tell her how much she was helping him. Though words seemed inadequate, they were all he had. He'd managed a few, only a few. She'd sent him one of those spine-tingling smiles, and he'd been sunk. Tongue-tied at thirty-two, Sam mused in disbelief.

More had happened, he recalled. He'd moved closer. Instead of telling her how glad he was she'd taken the job, he'd been wondering why he hadn't noticed before how long and dark her lashes were. How soft her mouth looked.

She would figure this out, Jessica told herself. How hard could it be to wash clothes? She dumped the clothes into the machine and stared at the dials. ''Gentle cycle? Heavy?'' She lifted a small door on the top of the machine. ''Is this where the soap goes?'' More importantly, where is the soap? she wondered, looking around. Next to the machine was a cabinet. She started opening and closing doors.

''The soap is here,'' Casey said, suddenly materializing beside her. She opened a lower cabinet door.

''And that's the button to start it,'' Annie said in her most knowing tone.

Jessica managed to get the load started with her two helpers nearby before they ran off to watch their favorite cartoon. She was so pleased with herself that she settled on a kitchen chair to read the morning newspaper while the clothes washed.

Half an hour later, no longer hearing the swishing and rushing water sounds of the washing machine, she hurried to it.

Her first thought was what had she done wrong as she frowned at the sock in her hand. She'd bet the Walker fortune that Sheriff Sam Dawson didn't own a pair of pink socks. So how did they get this way?

''Oh, oh.''

Jessica swept a look over her shoulder to see Annie's mouth still shaped in a perfect *O*.

Beside her, Casey's eyes were wide as she stared at the pink sock.

"What did you do?" Annie asked accusingly.

Casey continued to chew on her bottom lip.

"I don't know." Jessica's voice trailed off as she spotted Casey's red shorts tangled in one of his T-shirts. As she folded a pale pink T-shirt she wanted to cry. He was going to fire her.

By dinnertime, Jessica had exhausted herself cleaning the house, hoping he'd see what a good job she'd done and keep her. And despite the disaster in the laundry room, she really had a wonderful day with the girls. In one short afternoon, she'd been absolutely charmed by their loving, bubbly personalities.

Still in her nonstop, jabbering mode, Annie skirted the table and set down silverware as Jessica had requested, then quite suddenly announced that she and Casey were looking for a mommy.

Jessica paused spooning coffee grounds into the brewing basket of the coffeepot and gave them her full attention. Were these two angelic-looking girls really discussing finding a woman for their daddy?

Jessica listened as they spieled off their choices.

"I don't like her," Casey said simply about one woman.

Jessica bit back a smile as Casey wrinkled her nose in disdain.

"Who don't you like?"

They all swung around.

Sam stood in the doorway. Jessica watched him run

a hand through hair glistening with moisture, then glanced at the window. "It's raining?"

"Started a few minutes ago." He touched the top of Casey's head. "So who don't you like?"

"The lady with the real *black* hair," she said honestly.

Looking puzzled, he inclined his head to see his daughter's face more clearly. "Michelle Ranchet? You don't know her."

"She likes you."

Understanding snapped in his eyes. "Don't worry about it, Casey." He ran his large hand over her hair. "Okay?"

A thoughtful look kept her smile at bay for only a moment. "Okay."

His gaze shifted to Jessica. "Would you do something for me?"

Caught up in the softness of that moment between him and his daughter, a second passed while what he'd said registered. Instinctively, she tensed over words similar to ones she'd heard too often. *"Do this for me, Jessica." "Use your family influence for me." "Help us with a donation." "Talk to your grandfather for me."*

"Do you want to?" Sam asked.

It took a second for her to answer. She met his eyes with a puzzled expression. "I'm sorry. Do I want to what?"

"To make the vegetables?"

Make vegetables. She nearly laughed. This is a different world, she reminded herself. This man is different. Relax. He doesn't know who you are. "Yes."

There was no reason not to trust him. Another man had broken her heart. Nathan had taught her a lesson about trusting too easily. But she wasn't seventeen anymore. She wasn't gullible. More importantly, this man couldn't want anything from her. He didn't know who she really was.

Jessica raised her gaze, saw Annie heading for the door. "You have time until dinner," she said to her. "To do what we talked about."

"Oh, yeah." Annie grabbed her sister's hand. "Come on."

Sam shut the refrigerator door and held out a tomato. "What's going on?"

"They're making get-well cards for Mrs. Mulvane."

"Your idea?"

Jessica took the tomato, was slow to answer. Did he disapprove? "Well—yes. Is that okay?"

Facing the cupboard, his words came out muffled. "It's nice. Thanks." He stepped back, held out a cutting board. "Casey likes tomato slices," he explained.

As his fingers brushed hers, in an instant, with that simple touch, warmth came to mind. A sense of strength. And an undeniable and unexpected surge of pleasure.

"I should have thought of the cards. Arlene will love them."

"I hope so." She produced a weak smile for him while she told herself she was being silly. She was too old for such a reaction to his slightest touch. Consciously she concentrated on the tight muscles in her shoulders while she hunted in first one cabinet, and then another for plates. Talk. If they kept talking, she would relax.

"What do you need?"

"Plates," she said, opening another cabinet.

"Next one over."

Tomorrow she would poke around so she knew where everything was.

"Did you have a good day together?"

"Yes. I learned they're very different."

"They sure are." Pride came through clearly in those few words.

"I mean really opposite," Jessica said lightly. She'd learned that Annie loved dresses and that Casey hated them. She learned that purple was the only color in Annie's world, and that Casey loved green, because bugs liked grass and grass was green. Sam's tomboy, the bug-loving Casey ranked riding her bike as her favorite pastime. Annie preferred tea parties, viewed her doll as another member of the family, and coddled Casey during disputes. While they disagreed on a lot of things, they both declared chocolate chip cookies their favorite.

Jessica related well to both girls. She'd been just like Annie. She'd loved new dresses and tea parties with her dolls, and she'd consumed any book she could get. While time spent with Annie was easy, Casey snagged her interest. Probably because she was allowed to do all the fun things Jessica had only thought about as a child—climb trees, make mud pies, wear her favorite jeans everywhere.

"What was happening when I came in?"

A second passed before she recalled the conversation. "They were talking about their choices for a mommy."

She thought she heard him groan. "Do I want to know more?"

Jessica couldn't help laughing. "They decided against Angela."

Sam pivoted around, looked interested. "Angela—the waitress?"

"Yes, the one at the diner."

"I can hardly wait to hear this." Sam slouched against the refrigerator. "What's wrong with her?"

"She chews gum all the time. Too loudly, according to Casey."

Sam's smile widened. "Go on."

"And Annie says that the librarian tsks all the time."

"Accurate observation. She does. So they've ruled out Angela and the librarian."

"And the lady—the one with *real black* hair. The one who sells houses. Casey's words, not mine," Jessica was quick to point out.

"Michelle Ranchet."

Jessica nodded. The sexy-looking Realtor had strolled into the diner on Jessica's lunch shift and garnered her share of attention.

"Why do they object to her?"

"Her hair's too phony, Casey said. And she wears really high heels. But it seems her biggest offense is that she calls Casey sweetie."

On a chuckle, Sam moved from his position against

the refrigerator. Turning, he opened it. "Did they tell you who was on their 'okay' list?"

She shook her head. "Should I make a salad, too?"

He removed a package of thawed steaks from the refrigerator.

"If you insist." Over his shoulder, he smiled at her, then stepped back, holding the refrigerator door open wide as if in invitation. "In fact, if you want, I'll leave meal planning to you."

She would really love to do the planning. "I'd like to."

"Great. I'm not crazy about kitchen duty." In a distracted manner, he glanced at the window. Raindrops no longer pelted the glass. "The rain is easing up."

"Do you have to go back to work?"

"For a while."

People talked at the diner. They'd mentioned the sheriff. "The best we ever had," one of them had told her. A chatty man, he'd said that the sheriff worked too hard, buried himself in his job to avoid what was missing in his personal life. Jessica thought that might be true. People avoided the truth about themselves. Hadn't she done that, too?

Since the day she'd learned she was adopted, she'd done everything to please her mother. Why? That was a question she hadn't faced before this. But being alone, away from everyone, she'd had plenty of time to think. She knew now she'd never felt secure, was never sure her mother loved her, really loved her.

"I didn't tell you earlier," he said, grabbing her attention. "The house looks nice." He dug a carrot and a head of lettuce out of the vegetable crisper, then set them on the counter for her. "Really nice."

Jessica beamed. "Thank you." Pivoting, she opened the cupboard for a mixing bowl. She thought about mentioning the laundry, then decided against ruining the moment. Soon enough he'd find out what she'd done. "Did you always want to be a sheriff?"

"Not exactly that." Sam shut the refrigerator door and found himself only inches from her. Not for the first time, he caught a whiff of her fragile scent, and felt a craving curl in the pit of his gut. "I envisioned myself as a big-city cop, living dangerously all the time." When had the kitchen gotten smaller? Easing back, he waited until she moved away, then stepped up to the counter and yanked the cellophane off the package of steaks.

"Really?"

The way she said that one word made him turn toward her. She looked interested, really interested. In an honest second, he wasn't sure yet what he wanted from her. Time would tell. For now, it felt damn good to be in the familiar surroundings of his home with a woman who had no expectations about the evening, who only wanted to talk.

"Was your father in law enforcement?"

"I never knew him," he answered. "The tale is an old one." He waited until she finished scrubbing the vegetables, then he went to the sink and washed his hands. "My mother got pregnant. They married but he didn't stick around." Returning to the counter, he scored the edges of the steak. "After watching all she went through, I swore if I fell in love and got married, my kids would have a full-time father.''

He hadn't said that to sound like ''Superdad.'' He'd meant every word. He loved his girls, would die for them. He and Chris had been thrilled when she'd learned she was pregnant. He could still remember the night she'd conceived.

They'd made love by the fireplace that night. He'd stared at her flat belly beneath the glow of the flames, caressed her skin, kissed it, but had been unaware then how really precious a gift was inside her.

''So it was just the two of you?''

Looking up, Sam pulled himself from the memory. ''My mother died a week before my seventeenth birthday. Pneumonia. She was sick, but too proud. She wouldn't take time off from work.''

''Where did you go after she died?'' she asked and stopped slicing the tomato.

''I went to live with her brother.'' His gaze shifted to the French doors. Rain tapped lightly on the roof. Instead of talking, he should be outside on the patio lighting the charcoal. ''He wasn't the best influence. Arnie was Thunder Lake's town drunk.'' Sam doubted Arnie would have bothered with him if several townspeople including Thunder Lake High's principal, hadn't insisted, so Sam could finish high school in Thunder Lake. But Arnie never wondered where he was at night or how well he was doing in school. ''All he cared about was his next drink,'' he said aloud.

A memory floated back to him. Old Arnie during a drunken rage had taken a swing at him. Sam had sworn that he would never do that again. He'd grabbed Arnie's arm and wrestled him to the floor. It hadn't been hard. He was soft from too much drinking. At seventeen, Sam had stood eye-to-eye with him. Arnie had cussed him royally and told him he was no good. "One time he told me that my mother never wanted me."

Distress filled the blue eyes that focused on him. "That's terrible."

He hadn't said that for sympathy. The words had slipped out because he'd thought the idea so ludicrous even back then. His mother had been loving, she'd been his world. "I never believed him. There had always been only the two of us. When she died, I didn't care about anyone or anything. Then I met Christina." When he'd least expected his life to turn around, it had. She'd been what he'd needed most. She'd been everything soft that had been missing in his life after he'd lost his mother.

His silence grabbed Jessica's attention. "How did you meet?" she asked, trying to see the depth of his grief. But there was no change in his expression. Had he trained himself to veil emotions, keep them at bay?

"In high school. I always knew she was around, but didn't think I was in the same league with her." A hint of a smile curled the edges of his lips as if he was amused by his own thought. "I wasn't. She was so sweet, so pure."

She looked up from shredding the carrot. "And you were...?"

Humor gleamed in his eyes. "One of the town's bad boys. But I'll never admit that to my girls."

The mood had shifted. Jessica was quick to grasp onto his lightness. "You don't want to ruin your good-guy image?"

His smile grew. "Superhero. According to them. But they're young and easily fooled."

She liked how easily he turned humor on himself. "How did you know you wanted to be in law enforcement?"

"Nothing else felt right. My mother always said be honest. She drilled that into me. Being a cop seemed like the most honest thing I could do. Done with that?" he asked about the salad bowl.

Quickly she scraped shredded carrots into it. "Yes, I—" She looked up, and froze. He stood so near. As his eyes flickered from hers to her mouth, emotion sprinted through her. Was he leaning closer? Was he going to kiss her? She hoped so. She swayed toward him, brought her lips closer. She was definitely ready. More than ready. She started to raise a hand to his face but stopped. From the corner of her eye, she caught movement, saw Annie wandering in.

"Can I go outside?" she asked.

"Stay on the patio." He wore a frown as he swung away, as he snatched up the package of steaks. "I'll put these on."

Jessica listened to the sound of the screen door closing behind him. She stretched for a deep breath, a calming one, and picked up the bag of frozen vegetables to cook. Had she been imagining everything, or had he nearly kissed her?

"Daddy makes the bestest steaks." Casey grinned at her. "Him cooks good." She'd said something similar when Jessica went out back by her and Annie. For a few moments before dinner, she'd played a game of tag with them on the patio.

"He cooks good," Annie corrected.

Casey thrust out her chin. "I said that."

A frowning Sam was spooning vegetables onto his plate. Jessica held her breath, waiting for his comment. The lima beans and kernels of corn were flattened, the carrots were orange blurs. Earlier when distracted by her own thoughts, she'd overcooked the vegetables. She felt terrible that she was making such an awful impression, especially since she'd considered cooking one of her rare domestic talents.

Across the table, Annie went on, "I'm going to be an elephant in my school play. It's on—" She paused, stared at the ceiling as if something was written there. "A Wednesday. Will you come, Jesse?"

She wondered if she'd still be here.

"Jesse?" Annie asked impatiently.

"If I can."

"Is the steak okay?" Sam asked between bites.

"It's wonderful."

"These are mushy." Annie curled her top lip at the vegetables on her plate.

"They taste fine," Sam said. "Eat them."

"That's my fault," Jessica admitted. "I overcooked them."

Both girls' heads swung toward their father then to her, then back to him as if they were watching a tennis match.

"I'm sorry," Jessica added.

"You don't have to apologize." Sam sent a meaningful look in the girls' direction. "They're okay. Good, in fact, aren't they?"

Though they hesitated first, they both nodded.

"They're okay," Casey said.

"The flavors blend this way," Sam added.

He was a nice man. He had to be to come up with that excuse so quickly.

"On Friday, I'm going to take my snake for 'share day,'" Casey declared suddenly after several minutes of eating.

Snake? What snake? Jessica darted an apprehensive look in Sam's direction.

"To scare him?" Annie asked.

Casey's head bobbed. "Uh-huh."

Head bent, Sam kept eating, looking unfazed by his daughter's announcement, though he asked between bites of food, "Who is *him?*"

"Harrison. He's a bully," Annie responded.

Casey's nose wrinkled. "He's not nice." Ceremoniously she set down her fork. "I'm done." A green bean clung to the tips of her fork. "Daddy, can we go watch television now?"

"Don't you have a math test tomorrow to study for, Annie?"

"On Tuesday, Daddy." Exasperation edged her voice. "I told you. She gives us a math test every Tuesday. She's a real hard teacher," Annie whined.

"Truly abused," Sam murmured on a laugh. With his nod of okay, they took their plates to the sink.

Jessica met them there and turned on the hot water

for dishes. "Is there really a snake?" she asked once the girls had left the room.

Standing, he looked at the galley-style clock on the wall above the sink. "A rubber one. Had you wondering for awhile, didn't they?"

She laughed, pivoted back toward the table to get the rest of the plates and nearly plowed into him. Instinctively her hand flew out, flattened against the hard plane of his chest. Standing only inches from him, she felt her heart flutter, felt his pound harder.

"We have to stop meeting like this." He smiled, laughed as if at himself then stepped back.

He said something about a town council meeting and a goodbye to the girls. Nodding, she presented her back to him and made much about folding a dish towel until she was sure he'd left the kitchen. She'd felt it again, that swift, unmistakable rush of pleasure.

Nerves tight, she ran water in the sink and began sudsing dishes. She liked doing the task. Liked the quiet time. Mostly she liked the soothing sensation of her hands in the soapy water. At the moment, she needed something to soothe her.

Rinsing the last plate, she dried off her hands and wandered out of the kitchen and toward the living room, unsure if Sam had left yet.

She'd intended to check the driveway, see if the sheriff's car was gone, but on the way to the living room window, she passed his den and saw him. Jessica stopped in the hallway outside the door.

Sitting forward, he held a photograph in his hands and simply stared.

She was certain she hadn't moved, made a sound,

but in that way that a person knows another is near, he slowly angled a look at her.

"I didn't mean to intrude," she said quietly.

Standing now, he set the photograph back on his desk. Jessica had seen it earlier. It was of a woman with light-brown hair and dark-blue eyes, pretty enough with her bright smile to be a model in a toothpaste commercial.

"Annie looks like her," he said quietly.

What could she say? "She was beautiful."

"Yes," he said softly, then looked away from the photograph of his late wife. His loss echoed on that one word.

Jessica's heart tugged for him. She'd known a similar emptiness for months after her grandmother had died. She wished for him what she'd finally found to overshadow the grief—wonderful memories of her lost loved one.

"Be careful," she said now as he neared where she stood in the doorway. For the sake of the two little girls in the other rooms, she worried about him.

"I usually am," he offered as an assurance.

And so would she be. If she hadn't known the truth before, she knew it now. He was still mourning his late wife.

At nearly ten that evening, Sam left the library and the meeting with the town council. Inevitably it always included complaints about someone's dog barking, a teenager's boom box, or a too-noisy car engine.

With luck, the town's upcoming rummage sale would pass without any arrests, but he didn't really believe luck controlled his life. If it did, he'd have never suffered through one of life's agonies—losing the woman he'd loved.

Like earlier, rain beat against the window of his sheriff's car. Between the swish of windshield wipers, he squinted at the parking lot of a convenience store, saw nothing to investigate, and kept driving.

It was almost midnight by the time he returned to the house. Not tired, he checked on the girls. Sleeping, her eyes squeezed tight, Casey clung to her favorite stuffed animal. He bent over her, kissed her lightly. In response, her nose twitched and her little fingers clutched tighter around the neck of the green ant. It hung half off the bed.

Sam pushed its legs up and under the blanket, and then he kissed Casey again. Smiling, he wandered into Annie's room. She was curled on her side. Her lips slightly parted, she looked as if she was smiling. Gently he kissed her.

"Good night, Daddy."

Sam stroked back her bangs. "Good night, sweetie." Anything bad in his life disappeared for him during the moments when he said good-night to them. He lingered a little longer, waiting until she was drawing the deep breaths of sleep again, then left the room and wandered through the dark hallway.

He hated nights like this when tiredness eluded him, and there was no one to talk to.

Stepping into his room, he yanked his shirt from his pants. He considered going downstairs for a beer. He unbuttoned his shirt, shrugged out of it, and then forgot the idea. He didn't really want the beer. He wanted someone to talk to. He wished Jess—

Jess? How quickly she'd slipped into all their lives. He understood the girls needed womanly softness. Perhaps that was his problem, too. Maybe all that he was feeling now was because he'd seen those long legs encased in snug jeans chasing after Casey in a game of tag before dinner. Maybe it stemmed from seeing that rich-colored auburn hair flying beneath the caress of the wind when she tossed back her head with laughter. Maybe this came from nothing more than the slow, easy curve of her lips when she smiled.

Whatever the reason, the result was the same. This was about chemistry. And maybe, he reflected, it was time to think like one of the living again.

Spotting his folded laundry on the dresser, he crossed to it. It was nice of her to do the laundry. He wasn't sure she would do— He stared hard at the T-shirt. At a pair of socks. At all his socks. Pink.

Everything was *pink.*

What had she done? On a burst of laughter, he dropped to the edge of the mattress. He could imagine the looks his deputies would give him. Hell, who cared. So his socks were pink, it just felt so damn good to laugh again.

Chapter Six

He laughed often during the next week, he realized. He never mentioned the pink underwear to her, not wanting to hurt her feelings. He solved that problem with a few new purchases. But a growing attraction for her proved more difficult to handle. He definitely wasn't immune to her, to those eyes that a man could drown in. And this morning he was feeling impatient to see them.

With a glance at the kitchen clock, he went to the sink, looked out the window. She'd gone for her morning run half an hour ago.

Frowning, he dropped bread in the toaster, then returned to the ironing board. Behind him, sitting at the kitchen table, the girls chattered.

"Are we waiting for Jesse?" Annie asked.

"No, you go ahead," he said, sharper than he intended. Quickly he sent a smile toward Annie to banish her frown. Annoyed with himself, he shoved the iron harder over the front of his shirt.

Jessica jogged a final corner and headed toward the house. This morning, she'd awakened thinking about Casey.

Before falling asleep last night, the little one had, in a confidential manner, leaned her head close to Jessica's. "I don't really like them," she'd whispered about a pair of green sneakers she owned. "But my daddy bought them."

Jessica smiled at the memory while she filled her lungs with the cool morning air. She'd become a confidante, she'd been trusted with the secret that Casey would wear the shoes rather than hurt her father's feelings.

Who knew better than she just how important trust was? She, too, had a secret, and though she still lacked the faith in anyone to tell it, a closeness had begun with Sam and his daughters. Each day with them drew her deeper into their lives. She couldn't be indifferent, couldn't simply pretend this was a job. She'd begun to bond with them.

"Morning," a voice yelled.

Raising her head, she returned the greeting as she passed another early-bird jogger. Across the street, a neighbor waved. She'd never lived in a close-knit community before. Home had been her grandfather's mansion in Willow Springs, or his villa in Spain, or his estate in Florida, places where she'd been surrounded by everything she could want. Places where she'd felt terribly alone.

Slightly winded, she slowed her stride when she neared the back door of Sam's house. That aloneness was of her own making, she knew, reaching for the doorknob. But it was safer to question someone's interest in her than to trust them. Wasn't that why she really liked being here? Without the name Walker attached to her, she could believe in the people around her, not search for ulterior motives in anyone who was nice to her.

"Hi, Jesse," chirped Casey.

"Hi." She thought she'd answered the little one, might even have smiled a greeting, but wasn't certain. She stood frozen at the door, her eyes locked on Sam. Naked to the waist, he stood at the ironing board. She didn't move, couldn't. It was definitely too early in the morning to see so much smooth, well-muscled flesh. When he turned to face her, her throat went suddenly dry.

"Morning. Coffee is made."

"Okay." She gave him her best I'm-not-looking-at-you-at-all look, but when he resumed ironing, she took a lengthy view of him. Forearms and biceps looked stone-hard. So did his midsection. Before he caught her still staring, in her best breezy and nonchalant manner, she ambled to the toaster, then shoved in two slices of bread. It wasn't as if she'd never seen a half-naked man before, she reasoned.

"I wanted you to know that you'd have time to yourself tomorrow evening. The girls are going on a sleepover."

She looked away from the popped toast to see him shrugging into the crisp, immaculately ironed shirt of his uniform.

"It's going to be lots and lots of fun," Casey assured her.

"I bet it will be." Listening to a command from her brain to move, she went to the sink and washed her hands. Without looking back, she knew he was busy folding the ironing board. It seemed when in a room with him that she was always aware of what he was doing. "You're all up early." She buttered the toast and took it to the girls. "I thought I'd be back before you came down for breakfast."

"Don't worry about it." Head bent, he finished buttoning his shirt. "Do you want to go to the grocery store today?"

Another first. Well, how hard could it be to shop for groceries? And she did love to shop. That was one of her favorite pastimes. "Okay."

"We have coupons," Annie said, looking up from her cereal.

Briefly Sam's eyes fastened on hers. He smiled. "I wrote down mostly staples. You add anything you need for meals."

She'd had a few ideas for special meals next week. So far her dinners had been successful. He'd raved about her breaded pork chops, chicken kiev, and fettucini alfredo. "Do you want anything special?"

"No. Anything you make will be fine." As he spoke, he withdrew his wallet from his rear pocket.

"Can we go, too?" Casey asked.

"You'll be at school. Morning preschool," he informed Jess.

She sent an appealing look at Jessica. "Couldn't you wait for us?"

Jessica saw no reason not to. "Sure. I'd like that."

Sam released a laugh that sounded more like a snort. "You have obviously never been shopping with kids. No matter what they ask for, the answer is no."

"Daddee," they wailed in unison.

"Daddee," he mimicked, his eyes soft with love.

Jessica smiled at the father-daughter exchange. He was a big man with strong-looking hands, and intense eyes, but when he stared at one of his daughters or talked to them, he was all gentleness.

"Annie, get ready. It's almost time for your ride. We'll go, too, Casey," he added.

While she dashed out of the room, Annie planted her feet. "I am ready," she assured him.

"Usually one of Annie's friends—"

"Stephanie is my best friend," Annie told her.

"Her best friend's mother," he said, receiving Annie's smile, "usually drives Casey, too, but the woman has a dentist appointment this morning, so I'll take her."

"I could drive Casey this morning," Jessie said.

"I'd like to let you. I'm rushed this morning, but I promised I'd drive her."

"I can't go yet." Casey charged in, looking devastated. "I can't leave until I find my red purse."

The infamous red purse, Jessica mused. "We'd better search for it."

She heard Sam's sigh, sensed he wanted to suggest

that his youngest leave without it. Instead he started
for the doorway to begin looking. "We'll have to find
it soon, or you might have to forget about it, Casey."

She wailed a plea. "Daddy, please."

Jessica took off for the living room. Where was the
last place Casey had been with the purse? Last night
she'd been watching television with Annie. Jessica
eyed the upholstered chair in the corner of the room.
Sticking out from under the cushion was a thin, red
strap. How had they missed seeing it? she wondered
while she lifted the cushion for it.

Her curiosity piqued, as she ambled toward the
kitchen, she slowed her stride, opened the clasp and
peeked inside. She'd expected treasured possessions
like a barrette or a comb in the wallet-sized purse.
Instead it contained stones and dead bugs. "Ugh."

"Ah, you peeked."

Startled, she jumped, spun around and found herself face-to-face with Sam. He stood near, so near his
breath warmed her face when he peered inside the
purse. "Have you seen what's inside it?" she asked
lightly to steer her mind elsewhere.

A grin cut a crease into his cheek. "Her collection
grows." He pointed at a butterfly. "I'm not sure why
she does this," he said, but there was something in
his eyes that told her it didn't matter. "Her preschool
teacher is helping her identify them. That's why she
was in such a panic."

In that moment, Jessica's admiration for him grew.
While he might have some expectations and enforce
some restrictions, he was raising independent free

spirits. Thinking back to how restrained her childhood had been, she envied the girls.

"I think it's her soft heart," Sam went on. "She feels badly that they're lying around, forgotten."

From the driveway, a car honked.

Jessica said the obvious. "There's Annie's ride."

"You know you saved the day," Sam told her. A simple movement, an inch closer, and she could be in his arms, he realized. "We'd have never gotten out of here without that purse." *Kiss her.* That one thought hammered in his brain.

"You found it!" Looking gleeful, Casey dashed from the doorway to take the purse dangling from Jess's fingers.

With no other choice, Sam let the girls dominate the next few moments. "Jess found it," he said.

Jubilant, Casey sent Jess one of her closed-lip grins that rounded her face. "Thank you, Jesse." Her red purse slapping against her side, she raced toward the door. "I'm ready, too, Daddy."

Whatever he'd planned seemed only a kernel of a thought now. He started to turn away. He had to leave, drive Casey to preschool, but despite the thought, a tug-of-war still played out inside him. "I'll be right there, Casey," he said and spun back to face Jess. "Go and say hi to Stephanie." This moment seemed inevitable with her. He reached out, touched her face, felt the pulse at her throat quicken. "How many times am I not going to do this, Jess?"

He watched her eyes widen, darken. "This?"

"This." He lowered his head, brought his mouth close, but gave her time to step away. He needed to know if one kiss would end his preoccupation with her. "This," he said low, only brushing his mouth across hers, once, then again as if testing.

Beneath his lips, she sighed. It was all the encouragement he needed. Crowding her, he placed a hand at the back of her neck, held her still. Then he pressed his lips to hers. He'd planned a quick kiss, a sampling. In seconds, everything changed. She was sweet, so damn sweet. And the warmth of her willing mouth was more than he'd expected.

As need spiked through him, he pressed his mouth harder against hers, wanting more, longing for a deeper taste. He wanted to lose himself in her. Instead of satisfying, her sweetness intensified his craving.

"Daddy!" Annie's voice from the other room penetrated the beginnings of a passionate fog.

It took a moment, a long, difficult moment. He hadn't known how hard it would be to let her go. Slowly he straightened his back, raised his head, his mouth. He held her upper arms, driven by a need not to lose contact with her.

"Sam."

He heard her draw a shaky breath, stared into eyes soft with desire. "Do we need to talk about it?"

"Do we?"

"If you regret it," he said softly, an urge to crush her to him a breath away.

She looked vulnerable, uncertain.

"No, do you?"

Her answer made him smile. "Only that I didn't do it sooner." He pulled back then. Now he could go. "Later," he said.

Jessica thought her legs might buckle. Watching him leave, she sat on the arm of the sofa. She heard the door close behind all of them. What was she doing? she thought with incredulity. Good sense warned her that involvement with him was a mistake. She knew better. This was temporary. She wouldn't stay.

Her mouth still warm from his, she stood up and headed upstairs. She'd been truthful. She had no regrets. She'd been yearning for his taste. Still was.

But she'd thought it would be simple to stay with them, to work for him, and despite an obvious attraction, to keep everything casual. That had all sounded so sensible. But when he'd been holding her, when his mouth had been on hers, she hadn't thought about anything except the heat spiraling through her.

If this was only about desire, but it wasn't. Something was happening to her when she was with him that had nothing to do with passion. She didn't put a name to that feeling. Nothing she'd find with him could go anywhere. Eventually she would have to go home where she belonged.

Maybe she needed a tangible reminder that this was all momentary. Maybe she should call home, make contact with her mother. But what would she say?

That question plagued her even later when she was strolling toward town. What words would make a difference? If she couldn't convince her family, if she wasn't free of more pressure to marry Ryan, she vowed that she wouldn't go home.

"Jess!" Following the sound of the voice, she saw Cory hurrying from across the street and mentally winced that she hadn't kept a promise to call her.

Cory breezed past Jessica's apology. "Forget it. You were busy. I couldn't believe it when I heard you got a job taking care of Sam's daughters." Cory's hand gripped her arm with both affection and enthusiasm. "How do you like it?"

Jessica offered a self-depreciating grin. "I'm much better at being a nanny than a waitress. Do you have time for coffee?"

"I'd love to." Cory wrinkled her nose. "But not at Herb's."

For the next hour, over coffee at a nearby fast-food restaurant, she and Cory talked about her wedding plans, laughed about Jessica's experiences with the girls, and before they parted, they promised to keep in touch.

Alone, Jessica couldn't stall any longer, and made herself head toward the phone booth.

Sam neared the lake. With his car window open, he smelled the dampness on the air, but he felt the warmth of spring in the breeze. He and Christina used to drive to the water, sit under the stars and talk about their future, growing old together. Because of his job, he believed his fate might rest in the hand of a strung-out perp who was trigger-happy, and she might face that future alone.

Instead he was the one. He'd never expected it. He hated it. For months after her death, he'd felt such heaviness in him, it took all the energy he possessed to simply get out of bed. But he'd had no choice. He'd had the girls depending on him.

They'd survived, he thought with some satisfaction.

In fact, lately it seemed as if they were doing better than that—and so was he.

Driving away from the lake, he thought about the morning, about the kiss. He didn't know if Jess had been any more prepared for it than he had, but he'd reached his limit. Too many times he'd been close to her, had casually touched her and wanted to draw her into his arms. What he should do now was the problem.

Feeling uncharacteristically uncertain, he swore, not pleased with his ambivalence. He zipped his cruiser around one corner and then another to patrol the town's business district, three square blocks of an assortment of shops.

Beyond the center of town, a strip mall existed with a chain discount store. Squinting against the glare of the sun, he scanned the parking lot, cruised by slowly, saw nothing to stop him.

He'd passed the lot, started to negotiate a left turn to return to the office, and almost gave himself whiplash with a sudden look back.

One second passed. With a quick flick of his turn signal first, he veered sharply to the right and zipped into the parking lot toward the woman standing in the phone booth.

Armed with five dollars in coins, Jessica made herself call home.

As she'd hoped, Emily, the family maid, answered, "Oh, Miss Jessica, everyone is so worried about you."

"I didn't want to alarm anyone," she said truthfully. "Please tell them that I'm fine."

"Mr. Noble was here one day and quite upset."

Jessica felt discouraged. She'd hoped Ryan wouldn't still be interested. "Just tell everyone that I'm fine."

"You're not coming home, Miss?"

"No, not yet." And she didn't know when, she realized as she set the receiver back in its cradle. Head down, thoughts elsewhere, she turned around and found Sam only a few feet from her, lounging against his cruiser. Her heart thudding harder, she straightened her back. How long had he been there? Had he heard very much?

"Jess, you can use the phone at home anytime you want."

Slowly she moved closer to him. "Thank you." But of course, she wouldn't—couldn't. If he saw a phone bill to Willow Springs, Nevada, he'd only need to make a few calls and he would know her secret.

Perhaps it was her quietness that gave her away, or maybe he was becoming attuned to her moods. Whatever the reason, he inclined his head and stared at her as if determined to see what wasn't visible. "If something is wrong, if you need help, I'm here."

Jessica mustered up a semblance of a smile. "Thank you." She knew he meant that, but no one could help. And she couldn't share her dilemma with him. Possibly her family had done something outrageous like file a missing persons report. It didn't matter that he'd kissed her, that he might want her. He'd told her about himself as a boy, one who'd grown up being taught that honesty mattered most. If her family had notified the authorities, wouldn't he, as sheriff, feel honor bound to inform them where she was? "Everything is all right." She tensed, expecting uncomfortable moments because of more questions, because of a kiss.

"Sam," a feminine voice called out.

Jessica sighed with relief at the sight of the woman crossing the street. With her approach came a reprieve. "A friend?"

He'd yet to look away, she realized. "I'm yours, too. Remember that."

How much she wished she could confide in him.

"Aren't you going to introduce me?" the woman was asking.

Jessica zeroed in on the woman now standing beside Sam.

Tall and brunette, wearing jeans and a heavy quilted vest, she was pretty, with an oval-shaped face, enormous brown eyes and a bright friendly smile. And from nowhere, as the woman smiled at Sam, Jessica felt a twinge of emotion that bordered so close to jealousy she was shocked to feel it.

A laugh crinkled faint lines out from the corners of Sam's eyes. "This is the unbashful Liz Lewis," he said lightly and completed the introduction. "Liz lives across the street."

Jessica presented a smile while trying to gauge the relationship between them. "Hi."

"I noticed you're staying at Sam's."

"Don't be subtle, Liz," Sam teased. "Ask if I'm having a thing with her."

"Quit it!" She sent him a pseudo glare.

Looking amused, he informed her before the moment got out of hand, "She's the new nanny."

Jessica was grateful that he'd clarified everything. She'd felt the beginnings of a blush rushing over her face.

Dark brows veed over the woman's dark eyes with her frown. "Where's Mrs. Mulvane?"

"You didn't hear?" he asked. "She had a heart attack."

"How awful." She looked genuinely concerned while Sam explained what had happened. "I'll have to give her a call." As she spoke, she glanced at her wristwatch. "I have to run. But it's nice to meet you, Jess. Let's get together some morning."

"I'd like that," Jessica responded. The friendship being offered spurred another pang of guilt. So many people were accepting her at face value, and though she hadn't lied, she had deceived them.

"She meant that," Sam said once they were alone again. "She'd be a good friend if you're looking for one."

Never had she expected to find so much here, including new friends. It seemed inevitable that she'd feel a truckload of regret later. "You've known her a long time?"

Suddenly he slipped a hand beneath her elbow. "Since I was a kid."

She felt the pressure of his fingers, felt him propelling her toward the street. "Is it my imagination or are you kidnapping me, Sheriff?"

Laughter rose in his throat. "Have you ever been

to the ice cream parlor? Tourists come from across the country to go to MaryLou's Ice Cream Parlor.'' He made it sound as wonderful as a day at Wimbledon or a weekend at St. Moritz.

Like a lifeline, she grabbed at the light-spirited mood he was forcing on them. ''Do they?'' She traced his stare to the quaint building with its red and white striped awning.

''Sure they do. Come on, I'll buy you a sundae. Schooner size,'' he added. ''Sugar wafers included.''

Having expected more questions, she was grateful for the levity. ''How could I resist?'' she said with another laugh.

Charming best described the ice cream parlor, with its red-and-white peppermint-striped, cushioned seats; white, wrought iron furniture and old-fashioned soda fountain.

Sam ushered her to one of the tables for two. Within minutes, Jessica was savoring the taste of rocky road ice cream smothered with hot fudge sauce, whipped cream and nuts.

''Good?''

''Hmmm.'' She licked at the spoon. ''This is a chocoholic's nirvana.''

He laughed and shoved his spoon into a strawberry concoction. ''My mother always said that chocolate was food to soothe the soul.''

''That sounds like something my grandmother would say. She had all kinds of silly little sayings.''

He stretched his legs beneath the table. ''Like what?''

A fond memory flashed back at her. "I remember once when I was worrying that I wouldn't be invited to a birthday party. I was about eleven, and certain my life would end if I was the only one who didn't get an invitation. She told me, 'don't paint the devil on the wall.' You know, don't look for trouble that isn't there," Jessica added. "Especially since I had three weeks to get an invitation. But I was certain that I wouldn't get one."

"Did you get an invitation?" He stared with a quiet intensity that made her feel she needed to say more.

"Yes, I did."

"She was right then."

"Always. She was my rock." She stared down at his strong hand so near hers. He, too, was the kind of person another could lean on.

"She was a strong woman?" he asked.

Jessica knew the question was leading her, but still responded. "Yes, but she was also soft and so gentle." And Jessica knew she'd puzzled the rest of the family. At times her grandmother had been painfully honest. Often she'd put Jessica's mother and grandfather down a peg.

When Deidre had grandiose ideas, her grandmother squelched any pretentious scheme with a few words. She'd have understood Jessica's present plight and comprehended why she was trying to stand on her own and get control of her life. Her grandmother would have encouraged her to flee this preposterous arranged marriage. "It's funny how a sad moment sometimes gives a wonderful memory."

Caught up in the recollection, she set down her

spoon. "The day after my grandmother died, my grandfather took me fishing. I'd never gone before. We didn't talk very much, but I felt my grandmother watching us, smiling down on us." They'd gone one more time when she'd been thirteen and her mother had been in Paris on a buying spree. Upon returning home, she'd learned about the trip and been enraged that her daughter was doing something so provincial. Jessica had never gone with him again.

"Were they paternal grandparents?"

She wasn't sure why she was discussing her family. But she'd been so restrained, so unable to talk to anyone about the people who mattered to her. Maybe because he trusted her with his children she felt he deserved to know something about her. "Yes. I never knew my mother's parents. In fact, I never knew my mother, my real mother." She frowned at the melting ice cream in the schooner glass. Why had she said that?

Questions flashed in his eyes. "Your mother died?"

"This is kind of complicated," Jessica answered. How much should she tell him?

"I have plenty of time," Sam responded.

No evasive move would work. He was silent, disturbing—waiting. She had to tell him what she meant. "The woman I think of as my mother adopted me." That wasn't something her family discussed. She'd learned the truth when she was seven, and no one had ever mentioned it again. "After my father died, his wife learned that one of my father's lovers, a Las Vegas dancer, was pregnant." She planned to stay as close to the truth as possible without giving her identity away. "I was what they called a love child. Anyway his wife—the woman I think of as my mother—adopted me."

Sam arched a brow. "It takes a special woman to want the child of her husband's love affair."

"I think she needed some reminder of him." Jessica knew that in her own way, Deidre loved her. But she always wondered why she'd adopted her, why she'd been willing to take another woman's child. She'd begun to wonder if Deidre's generous act had stemmed from a more selfish need to stay in favor with Jessica's grandfather and the Walker fortune. Having lost his son, her grandfather needed someone. Beneath his hard-nosed, business demeanor, Stuart Walker possessed an enormous soft heart. He would have accepted any child of his son's.

"Jess?"

She blinked, snapping herself from thoughts, saw Sam's brow had furrowed with a questioning frown.

"Your father died before you were born?"

"He was killed in a plane crash."

She raised her eyes to see his narrowing and knew instantly what she'd done. Plane crashes, commercial plane crashes, were newsworthy. Private planes usually belonged to the affluent.

He proved predictable. "In a commercial airplane?"

"No." Tensing, she straightened her back. "It was a company plane." She wasn't lying. "He was flying across country on business." Jessica didn't add that it was her father's private plane.

"Did you ever want to meet your real mother?"

So many questions, she mused. "No," she answered. It always bothered her that her birth mother hadn't wanted her. She supposed that sense of abandonment was the emotional baggage of an adopted child. Regardless, she never wanted to meet her. Why should she? The woman had left her, hadn't she?

Jessica met his stare squarely. He was good, she decided. He'd brought her here, relaxed her, asked a few questions, didn't push, and she'd talked freely. She'd said far more than she'd intended. "Thank you for the ice cream." She tried to make light of the moment. "I bent your ear, didn't I?"

"I was curious."

She met his stare. "I know. Why?"

"Because you say so little."

She wanted to sound steady, but her pulse mocked her as it raced at an uneven pace. "Is that inquisitive streak why you became a cop?"

"I like to solve puzzles." He broke into a smile. "Did you grow up in Nevada?"

"In a small town." A half truth. Willow Springs with its acreage and affluent homes was neither rural America nor big city. "Do you think I'm a puzzle?"

"Truth?" He nodded. "I wonder what you're hiding."

She'd been unprepared for his bluntness.

His eyes prodded her to tell him more. "Who are you, Jess?"

Anxiety fluttered her heart. "Who am I?" Her mother always said she was quick on her feet. She laughed as if amused, hoping she'd keep him from more probing. "I—I'm an heiress."

Chapter Seven

Sam shook his head and grinned, not taking her seriously. "Right." But what he didn't know about her had bothered him. He didn't care if she thought this was none of his business. The cop in him hadn't been able to ignore signs that she was in some kind of trouble, but he couldn't drill her.

As she shifted on the chair, her knee brushed his beneath the table. Need churned within him. His blood warmed. He stared at her mouth. It was seductive, inviting. He wanted her taste again. Not for the first time when around her, he couldn't stay objective about her, couldn't think like a lawman. "Ready to leave?"

As if anxious now, she stood first and reached for her shoulder bag on the seat beside her. "No more questions?"

God, she had gorgeous eyes. "You'd dodge them, wouldn't you?"

An apologetic expression etched lines in her face. "I'm sorry."

"You want me to trust you?"

She looked pained. "Yes. I guess I do. I promise. I've done nothing illegal. I'm not dangerous." She offered a slim smile. "Or crazy." An appeal entered her voice. "I can't explain any more than that."

He thought she probably could, but wouldn't. Though he knew little about her, he'd learned that trust didn't come easily to her.

"I had a good time." Her smile widened. It was that toothy dimpled one that had nearly flattened him the first time. "Thank you for the ice cream."

At the door, he reached around her to open it. But he took a moment as her flowery fragrance drifted to him. When her eyes fastened on his, it occurred to him that all his thinking power might have sunk to below his belt.

"Sam, thank you."

With her touch on his forearm, he silently groaned.

"You already thanked me for the ice cream."

"Not for that."

"For what?" He played dumb simply because he wanted to keep her near a little longer. Unable to resist, he fingered a few strands of hair brushing her shoulder. They felt as silky as they looked.

"For—for being so understanding."

Understanding or gullible? Sam mused. He watched in fascination as one fiery curl coiled around his finger. All he knew was that he liked being with her, that he wanted her. And if they'd been alone and somewhere else, he'd have buried his face in her neck. He'd have kissed her. Hard. He didn't want some little peck, he wanted a long, hard, mind-dulling kiss. One that made her think about him when he wasn't near.

He wanted a lot more.

She'd told him the truth. And he hadn't believed her. That was her fault, Jessica knew. She'd deliberately answered him in a manner so he wouldn't believe her.

She didn't need to say more. She thought she'd said enough. With little effort, he'd drawn out memories and made her talk about things she'd never meant to say, had never uttered to another person. Yet she'd told him. In disbelief, she shook her head that she'd mentioned her grandmother, her mother, her birth mother.

Had she stayed with him much longer, what else would she have said? With parting words about seeing her later, he'd climbed back in his cruiser, answered another of Trudy's calls, and left.

Only then did she realize what time it was. Running late, she hurried to the house for the car, then sped toward the preschool to pick up Casey on time.

She made it there three minutes before school was over.

Wearing her usual big smile, Casey dashed to the car and talked excitedly while fastening her seat belt. ''I was a 'flag person' today.'' Proudly she pointed to the sticker of an American flag stuck on the front of her blouse.

Slowly Jessica negotiated out of the parking lot and into traffic. "Is that your favorite job?"

"That and being 'snack person.'" She looked out the window, then back at Jessica with a frown. "Where are we going?" she asked, indicating she was aware Jessica had turned right in the direction of town instead of left toward the house.

"Until it's time to pick up Annie, I thought we'd go to the library."

"Oh, good." Her face brightened. "Can I get books? Daddy let me when we went."

Jessica smiled at her enthusiasm. She gave Sam credit. He'd already fostered a love for reading in both girls. "We'll see," Jessica answered as she considered applying for a library card.

But she couldn't, she realized the moment she entered the library. To apply for a library card meant showing identification, letting someone besides Herb know her name was Walker. He may not have connected the name to Stuart Walker, but she doubted she would be so lucky again.

Instead she sat with Casey and read books to her until it was time to leave and pick up Annie.

Unlike her sister, Annie was frowning when she climbed into the car. Jessica looked in her rearview mirror. Annie's long face said it all, but Jessica asked anyway, "Did you have a good day?"

"Yes."

At the uncharacteristically succinct response from

Sam's chatterbox, Jessica felt she had to probe and learn why. "Annie, do you have a problem?"

"I have to make my elephant costume."

Jessica didn't understand why she was fretting about that. "For the play at school?" she asked, looking in the rearview mirror at her as she braked for a red light.

Casey matched her sister's worried frown. "Daddy won't know what to do."

Words flowed from Jessica's mouth before she could stop them. "Could I help?" Of course, she couldn't. Her sewing ability was nil.

"Would you?"

Seeing Annie's bright and hopeful face, she couldn't say no now. "Yes, I will." She hoped, really hoped, she could do this, and not disappoint Annie. Maybe it wouldn't be too difficult. "Is Stephanie in the play, too?" she questioned about Annie's best friend while easing the car into the grocery store parking lot.

"She's one of the elephants, like me."

"Don't worry about your costume." At that moment, she believed what she said.

With help from Stephanie's mommy maybe, just maybe, everything would work out.

As she hoped, Annie was back to normal. The rest of the way home, she talked about a story she'd read in school about a little girl's purple backpack.

By the time Jessica pulled onto the driveway next to the house, both girls were chattering about a new cartoon movie and had gotten Jessica's agreement to make chocolate chip cookies.

Together they hauled in groceries. While Jessica stored them, the girls took turns mixing the cookie dough. She listened to their giggles, and over a hot cup of tea, she contemplated Sam's birthday, making a list of people to contact.

To the girls' delight, the first batch of cookies came out of the oven looking perfect. Jessica left them munching on some and called Liz, who thought a surprise party was a great idea.

When Jessica telephoned Trudy, she acted thrilled at the idea of "putting one over on Sam." She promised to contact friends, and help with refreshments. Before the conversation ended, Trudy managed to expound on Sam's finer qualities. Jessica needed no one to tell her he was handsome, thoughtful and a great catch. She'd been having a difficult time not thinking about how easy it would be to fall hard for him.

With Trudy's cheery goodbye, she set the phone back in its cradle and was drawn to the girls' conversation because Casey sounded angry.

"It's not!" she yelled at her sister.

"It's dumb."

Casey argued back. "It's not."

"Yes, it is."

Casey looked crushed. "Uh-uh."

Before the disagreement escalated into a screaming match, Jessica cut in. "What is going on?"

Annie swung a look up at her. "It's dumb that she likes bugs."

"No, it isn't. She might be an entomologist."

Annie's pale brows veed. "An endo—what?"

"That's someone who studies insects."

Casey suddenly beamed.

Annie, too, looked impressed by the huge word and giggled.

Jessica was amazed at how easily they could be sidetracked.

"Do you want to be one of them, Casey?" Annie asked her sister.

"I don't know."

When her voice trailed off, Jessica looked up from sipping her tea to see delight flash in Casey's eyes.

"Daddy, Daddy!" She raced to him, and bubbled with excitement as he swung her up into his arms. "Could I be one of those en—en, bug people, Daddy?"

Sam had been standing in the doorway, watching them with their heads close. He'd heard his daughters' giggles mixing with Jess's softer, sultrier laugh, and a warmth that he'd thought he'd never feel again after his wife died had enveloped him.

Growing impatient for his attention, Casey tapped his shoulder. "Daddy, can I?" she repeated.

"Sure you can." Sam let his gaze take in the moment, the three of them, staring at him, smiling, and recorded it to memory before answering. "You can be whatever you want."

Looking pleased, she wiggled to get down. "Show him what we did, Annie," she said as her feet hit the floor.

"We made a surprise," Annie said proudly.

"A surprise?" The smell of freshly baked cookies hung in the air. Sam exchanged a smile with Jess. He felt a connection with her. It was the same intangible, man-woman link that he'd known with Christina when they'd shared a special moment about the girls, when something struck both of them as funny, when a look said as much as words. "Who's it for?"

"You," the girls said in unison.

"Me?" He laughed. "And what is my surprise?"

"Chocolate chip cookies. Your favorite."

"Whose favorite?" he teased.

Their giggles answered him before they scurried from the room.

Amused, he swung around to see Jess stretching for one of the blue coffee mugs hanging from the mug tree. "Did they harp at you to make the cookies?"

"It was no hardship. We had fun." She placed a cup of coffee in the microwave. "Did you have a busy day?"

How could she look so elegant in jeans and a T-shirt? "It was quiet."

In less than a minute, the microwave dinged.

"Two calls." He watched the swing of her auburn hair caught back in a bushy ponytail, wanted to touch. "The town council wants a deputy to be on duty to drive up and down the streets during the annual town rummage sale."

He nodded a thanks as she set the mug on the table for him.

"The other call came from a regular." Cup in hand, he blew at the steaming brew and moved to the kitchen doorway, so he could see what the girls were doing. By the sounds emanating from the television, his daughters were engrossed in the newest cartoon craze about pocket-sized monsters. "Clara Swamis complains weekly about all the cars driving by her place.''

Eyes he could get lost in turned on him with questions. ''She has a problem with people driving by?''

As he sidled closer, her scent drifted over him. ''Her house is on the way to the Thorensons.'' She smelled wonderful. ''I told her that there's no law to stop teenage boys from flocking around her neighbor's daughter, Thunder Lake High's femme fatale, Mandy Thorenson.''

He heard her short laugh before she opened a door of a kitchen cupboard. ''I'm sorry. I didn't think about dinner sooner.''

Dinner didn't matter. He'd like time alone with her, one-on-one time. ''Don't worry about it.''

''Daddy?''

With reluctance, his gaze moved to Annie standing in the doorway.

''Can we have pizza tonight?''

''Works for me.'' He crossed to the wall phone. ''Pepperoni?''

''Works for me,'' his youngest echoed.

Sam reacted with laughter. The phone in his hand, he stretched the cord to slip fingers around Jess's wrist. ''And you?''

She stilled in setting plates on the table. Beneath his fingertips, her pulse scrambled. The reaction pleased him. A few days ago, he wouldn't have admitted that. During moments alone, he'd tried to be rational. He reminded himself that he was the town sheriff. He was supposed to have his head on straight. He was a father. He was supposed to be responsible.

But damn, he was a man, too. Aching. And now instead of doing what he wanted, instead of taking her in his arms, he was asking her about pizza.

"Anything you choose is fine with me."

"What kind do you like?"

"Cheese."

"Half cheese, half pepperoni." Desire cut through him. He wanted to feel her naked, pressed against him. He wanted to hear her sigh with pleasure because he'd caressed her just right.

"I want a soda," Casey yelled at Annie.

"Don't push!" Annie screamed back.

As real life intruded, he blinked, focused, let the sounds of his daughters' voices raising in a squabble end a nice little fantasy. Peering into the refrigerator, they were shoving for position. "Stop now," he insisted. "Or no one gets any."

"I wasn't pushing," Casey said with a lift of her chin.

Sam veiled a smile at her indignant look. She was prepared to battle. Before she moved away, he caught her at the waist, dipped her back, then tickled her mid-section. Her giggles proved contagious. Not to be left out, Annie dived in, and Sam fell back with them to the floor.

Jessica watched for a moment, then swung away, making much about folding paper napkins in half. She loved taking care of the girls, and more often than not, she'd felt like a part of the family. But the sight of them like that forced a reminder on her. This was their life, not hers. For her own sake, the smartest thing she could do was maintain a more casual relationship with all of them.

She worked hard through dinner to keep conversation running about the girls and to avoid Sam's stare, hoping to block thoughts that might make her wish for more than what existed.

All went well, she reflected later, while dumping paper plates in the trash. The meal had passed with pleasantries and a relaxing casualness. They'd chatted about the town rummage sale and Trudy's interest in learning karate, and had listened to Annie ramble about the new bike Stephanie had gotten.

She expected Sam and the girls to disappear into the living room to watch a movie. Instead Sam remained in his chair.

Annie pushed back hers and impatiently stared at her sister. "You promised to play dolls," she said as Casey slurped the last of her drink through a straw.

Not looking thrilled, Casey returned a resigned sigh, and slurped one more time on the straw. "I'm coming. I'm coming."

Jessica waited for them to leave the room. "Casey is playing with Annie's dolls?" she questioned in disbelief. When Sam didn't answer right away, she looked his way. He stood at the sink, his back to her, but when he reached for a glass to wash, she noticed his frown.

"Periodically she humors her sister."

"Don't you wonder what Annie will have to do in return for Casey's agreement to play dolls?"

"She'll think of something," Sam responded. He wondered more why she'd been acting so different.

She'd responded when spoken to, laughed at the right moments, but she'd seemed distant and cool. Did this have anything to do with their time at the ice cream parlor? Though she hadn't been pleased about his questions, she'd been smiling when he'd left, had smiled, too, when he'd come in this evening. So what was going on?

"Daddy, Annie won't let me watch my cartoon," Casey yelled from the doorway.

Jessica whipped a look back over her shoulder.

Sam reacted more slowly. As if still caught up in his previous thought, he took a long moment, then stared at his daughter. "I'll be right there." His gaze shifted to Jessica. "I'd better get them settled in."

"Would you like me to help?" Jessica offered.

"Nope. I'll be back after I put them to bed."

A wave of depression floated over her. Whether he'd meant to or not, he'd sent a message loud and clear. The girls were his; he would handle them. They didn't need anyone else.

More upset than she wanted to be, she dumped the pizza box in the trash container, then began washing a few dirty glasses and silverware. She hadn't planned to meet someone who mattered. She'd never thought there would be any connection with the people she'd meet while away from home. She'd never expected two little girls to inch their way into her heart, or to find a man who'd spiral heat through her.

There had been only a few men who ever had. Nathan had been the first, and she'd been far younger nine years ago, far less experienced and terribly infatuated. Nathan had been just as taken—but not with her. He'd been in love with her family's money.

Not that what she'd found with Sam was love, she quickly reminded herself. But unlike the others, Sam didn't know that she was Stuart Walker's granddaughter, and he still showed an interest in her. Perhaps that's why she was really clinging to this phony identity, because it gave her freedom from the Walker name. It also gave her a new set of problems. By staying, she would get closer to them; she would probably be hurt.

She finished drying the last of the silverware and folded the dish towel. With time to herself, she settled at the kitchen table with the newspaper. She'd only scanned the horoscope and a comic strip when Casey bounded into the room.

"Jesse, I came to say good-night." Her last words trailed off as she threw her thin arms around Jessica's neck.

Jessica had barely returned the hug when Annie's arms replaced her sister's on her neck. She delivered a quick kiss on the cheek and spun away, too. "'Night, Jesse."

Not fair. How could she build up any resistance to that? She heaved a deep breath and swallowed against the tightness in her throat. She'd been feeling alone, and so left out until that moment.

"I had nothing to do with that," Sam said from his position in the doorway.

She blinked against the tears smarting her eyes, saw his smirk. "That was so nice of them, Sam."

"They insisted that they couldn't go to sleep until they said good-night to you."

I'm falling in love with your daughters, she could have said. In days, they'd filled her with their laughter and smiles, made her fret over their worries, and yearn for their hugs.

"Me, either," Sam said suddenly, quietly.

She wasn't certain what he meant, so she laughed to make light of the moment.

"Want to tell me what I've done wrong?"

You've done everything right, she could have told him. That's what was wrong. He didn't make it easy for her to keep her distance. None of them did. About the time she put up her guard, tried to be sensible, they grabbed hold of her heart again. "I cry when I watch greeting card commercials," she said on a sniff and hoped he'd accept the excuse and not ask more.

She didn't want to discuss them, or what her place was in their lives.

His eyes clouded with questions, but he shrugged. "So nothing is wrong?"

"No, nothing," she assured him with her best smile.

"Then have coffee with me on the porch."

Being alone with him with no chance of an interruption might be the riskiest thing she'd done so far. "I didn't finish cleaning up." She had, but could have made busy work, wiped the counter, cleaned the sink.

Holding the screen door open, he appealed, "Say yes. I need some adult conversation."

It wasn't his grin but the hint of exasperation in his voice that moved her. With no real excuse for refusing, she nodded. "Okay." Before she reconsidered, she grabbed her coffee mug and passed him at the doorway to lead the way to the swing. As she settled on it, she set her coffee on a small redwood table beside her. She could almost hear her mother speaking. *How quaint this is, Jessica.* Well, she thought it was lovely. The sound of crickets, the rustle of leaves and the clean, fresh smell really did please her. "It's nice out here."

"I like it." The swing squeaked when he joined her. "Sometimes I sit out here in the middle of winter."

In the distance, a coyote howled. Ranches constituted much of the land beyond the town. This was cowboy country. Maybe that's why she'd been drawn to the area. No flash, no neon. "What's your favorite thing to do?" she asked, knowing if she didn't keep conversation going, then she'd be tight against him, begging for a kiss.

He said nothing for a long moment, kept staring at her before he finally followed her lead. "That's easy." A smile came to his lips. "Fishing, with my kids, though I spend most of the time untangling their lines. They won't touch the bait and won't even think of keeping the fish. But they're great." Beneath his heeled boot, the porch floor creaked as he pushed at it. Gently the swing swayed. "It's warm and peaceful with the water lapping at the boat, and they talk constantly." Laughter warmed his voice now. "I can't think of any time I've had more fun."

She understood. That was how she'd felt when she'd gone fishing with her grandfather. "Is that one of the reasons you live here? Because of the lake and all that?''

In the darkness, he peered at her. ''All that?''

''Outdoorsy things.''

He gave her a smirking grin. ''No, we moved back here when Casey came along. Christina had a scare when we were living in Las Vegas.'' He stopped for a moment and looked up at the night sky. ''I was nearly shot one evening while chasing a perp in an armed robbery. After that she wanted us to go some place safer, so we returned to Thunder Lake.'' The remembrance aroused another. ''I thought about that later. We'd moved here so I'd be safe, and while visiting a friend, she was in a bus crash.''

A distant look slipped over his face as he went on. ''It was so strange. I'd been holding Chris, talking to her ten minutes earlier and then she was gone. The bus driver swerved to avoid a car that crossed the center line on the highway.''

Jessica drew in a hard breath. What could she say? His eyes remained so solemn and looked so serious. ''I didn't mean to bring up sad memories for you.''

''It's good for you to know what happened.'' The heat of his breath caressed her face. ''Sometimes the girls talk.''

This was about him, not them, Jessica mused. He put on a good show. Though he might be past deep grief, she felt its lingering wave. Quietly she spoke, not wanting to jar him back to her. ''I'm sorry, Sam.'' She really hadn't meant to open an old wound.

Lightly, as if touching something delicate and breakable, he brushed a knuckle across the slender line of her jaw. ''You are such a sweet woman.'' Gently but firmly his hands framed her face.

She stared into his eyes, dark beneath the shadowed light, and felt breathless. Nothing was happening as she'd expected. Feelings, so many feelings, swelled within her whenever she was with him. He was going to complicate her life, she knew that with certainty. No matter what happened from now on, she couldn't walk away and pretend she'd never met him.

A lightness, as if he was laughing at himself, laced his voice. ''Sometimes I can barely think straight when I'm around you.''

She was certain she stopped breathing. No man had ever said such a thing to her before. ''Sam—'' Her heart pounding, she watched his gaze lower, and she nearly licked her lips. The need to touch overwhelming her, she placed a hand upon his chest.

Then his lips slanted across hers. She wasn't sure what she'd expected, but it wasn't this slow-moving, knee-weakening kiss. She couldn't recall any man ever kissing her so thoroughly, with such tenderness.

Her head swimming, she curled her fingers in the front of his shirt as if she was clinging for her life. She heard a moan. Her own. Emotion led her. The more his lips twisted over hers, the more hers softened beneath his.

While he filled himself with her taste, she breathed in the clean male scent of him, was aware of her breasts tightening. And she trembled, wanting more. It was all so crazy.

She'd felt desire before, but the ground had never rocked beneath her. He weakened her legs. He heated her blood. He seduced her with a kiss. She felt him slide his hand beneath her shirt. A desperation swept through her as the warmth of his fingers cupped her breast, inched beneath her bra, found her nipple. Her body swelled with wanting. He could have taken her right there—now—she realized.

Yearning, she wavered between deepening the kiss or tearing her mouth from his. Before she couldn't pull away, she turned her face from his. She took only a moment to steady herself. Uncertainty about where they were going slithered through her. "I'd better go in and check on the girls," she said on a breathless rush.

"Jess." Her name came out softly, flowing sensuously off his tongue as she rushed from him. Sam wanted to call her back. He didn't. Consciously he listened to the click of her heels on the kitchen floor. Even as she put distance between them, her sighs echoed in his mind.

It didn't seem to matter that the cop in him wanted answers, wanted to know what she'd kept hidden from everyone.

Now with his arms empty and needs unsatisfied, he wished he hadn't let her go. During the kiss, desire had wrenched his gut. Since day one, he'd been drawn to this woman. Hell, say it like it is, he berated himself. She makes you feel alive. She makes you crave. Burn.

Chapter Eight

Jessica stood in the shower and prepared for a difficult moment or two at the breakfast table. She'd awakened to the sight of a dreary sky, promising rain. Her first thought was about Sam.

What would she do when she saw him this morning? How should she act? Slowly she descended the stairs. What if he wanted an affair? Was she ready for that? Oh, why had he kissed her like that, touched her? Why hadn't he left her sleeping desire rest?

Reaching the bottom stair, she heard a cartoon theme song she'd become familiar with since coming to Sam's house.

Annie, who loved a cartoon program with a big yellow bus that went on scientific excursions, sat in front of the television. With her legs folded cross-legged, she told Jessica that daddy had said goodbye minutes ago, but left her a note. On her belly, her chin cupped in her hands, Casey seemed just as engrossed in the television program.

So Sam, too, had anticipated difficult moments this morning? Was he deliberately avoiding her?

"Want me to show you the picture I colored?"

Jessica skimmed his note about Casey's preschool, then gave Annie her full attention.

"It's a butterfly," she said while holding up the drawing.

"That's very pretty, Annie."

Casey swung a look at the drawing. "Annie, that is so bad."

Bad meant good, Jessica had learned. As usual, they lifted her spirits. With a laugh, she left them and meandered into the kitchen to pour their cereal.

"I want the chocolate bears, Jesse," Casey said, trailing her.

"Already poured." She set a bowl of the dinosaur-shaped cereal on the table in front of her.

"Thank you. I like them best."

"I know." Jessica stroked the top of Casey's head and received her full cheek, close-lipped grin.

Only steps behind them, Annie perched on another chair. "Can I pour my own?"

"Sure you can." Jessica handed her the cereal box. A good portion spilled onto the table. Jessica pretended not to notice. For a few minutes, she listened to their excited chatter about their sleepover at their friend's house, then she wandered to Sam's den.

In his note, Sam had asked her to call Casey's preschool with the list of her immunizations. It's on my desk, he'd written on the note.

So was Christina's photograph.

Unable not to, Jessica studied it. She looked nothing like Christina, but had Sam been thinking of his wife when he kissed her? Was he hurting in a way that he grieved even when a smile curved his lips or a laugh slipped from his throat? How could she be certain that the kiss had nothing to do with feelings for Christina? Maybe she was a substitute for the wife he'd lost.

If any of that was true, he wasn't being honest with her. But while his dishonesty was unintentional, she couldn't say the same, and wondered if it wasn't best that nothing more had happened. How could she get involved with him and not be honest?

After calling Casey's preschool, she found the phone number for Stephanie's home in a black address book on Sam's desk and talked to her mother about the elephant costume. In the kitchen again, she made a sandwich for Annie's lunch, bagged it and an apple and was adding several packaged cookies just as Stephanie's mother beeped her car horn.

Hugs and kisses from the girls followed. Jessica stayed at the door long after they'd left. She'd never needed people around her. In fact, she'd been a bit of a loner. But with the quietness around her now, she felt so alone, missing the noise, and the turmoil, missing the children—and the man. Wise or not, she was beginning to treasure every moment with all of them.

She'd felt such joy when slim little arms had wrapped around her neck. She'd never thought about being a mother, or about children of her own. She assumed that one day it would happen, but unlike so many of her friends, she hadn't set out to be married before turning twenty-five. She'd believed marriage would come later for her. More important was finding a man who'd truly love her and not use her as a means to nurture his ambition or increase his monetary worth. Wasn't that one of the reasons she'd balked at marrying Ryan? She believed his reason for wanting to marry her had nothing to do with love.

With a sigh, she settled down with Annie's elephant costume. Though she lacked skill as a seamstress, every stitch she threaded on the costume was done with loving hands.

By the time she finished gluing the lavender cloth around the cardboard for the elephant's trunk, it was late afternoon. Satisfied with the job she'd done, she stood and stretched her back.

Having time to spare before she picked up Casey from her class, she snatched up the car keys. She'd been looking forward to driving around town, seeing the sights.

Squinting against the glare of an afternoon sun, she traveled along the two-lane highway that led out of town. It felt good to drive. Even though it was cool, she opened windows.

She'd heard talk while working in the diner. Some of the ranches surrounding the town were multi-million dollar empires. She enjoyed the sights—the distant pine-covered mountains, wide-open grazing lands, herds of sheep and cattle.

Nearly an hour passed before she circled back toward town. Nearing the lake, she lowered the volume on the radio. A peaceful quietness accompanied her on the drive along the lake road. Stopping near the water, she drew in a deep breath. The scent of fish wafted on the air. Nearby a jackrabbit scurried into a bush.

Unable to resist, she stepped out of the car, welcoming the feel of the wind ruffling her hair, the late afternoon chill.

Since he'd awakened, Sam had been wondering what to say to her that would make sense. This morning he'd dressed quickly, said goodbye to his daughters, and had left the house without seeing Jess. He reasoned that he seriously needed to think this through.

If he pursued her, what would she expect? He didn't want more than the moment. That's what no one seemed to understand. He wasn't ready to bond with any woman again. Maybe he never would be.

Cruising down the town's main street, he slowed when he passed Dugan's Bar. From the opened door, he heard nothing louder than the usual ruckus and kept driving.

"Sam, are you there or at the car wash?" Trudy's voice crackled over the radio.

"I'm here." He'd taken one look at a sky filled with clouds, and had known better. Every time he washed the dang thing it rained.

"Well, we got a problem. A call came in from Reno. There's an APB for a guy named Wilkins."

Sam made a mental note of the vehicle and license plate she'd rattled off.

"Wilkins is on the run from an armed robbery charge. They figure he's headed our way. He's got a cousin in Burns," Trudy said about a town a few miles east of Thunder Lake.

"I'll drive that way." He was willing to play highway patrolman for a while, watch for Wilkins's car, but he headed toward the lake first. "Contact Gary. Tell him to keep an eye on town—"

"Dugan's Bar?" she cut in.

"And Holden's Sporting Goods. I figure someone has a grudge against him."

"Will do."

"I'm driving around the lake area first." He'd already negotiated the turn onto the lake road. Isolated camping areas around it offered hiding places.

"Right," Trudy responded.

Her voice was lost to him. All thoughts slithered away. Bathed in the warm glow of sunlight, Jess stood near the water's edge, the wind blowing her auburn-colored hair away from her face, whipping at her blouse, her jeans, plastering the cloth against her.

He ached just looking at her.

In the midst of the quiet, it was the rumble of a car engine that drew Jessica's gaze away from the circling pattern of an eagle. With a turn, she saw Sam climbing out of the sheriff's car. Nerves danced within her. She wasn't certain what to say or how to act. Should she pretend nothing different happened yesterday? Was that possible? "Hi," she said as he drew near. Silently she groaned. Surely she could have come up with something more enticing than that. Uneasy, she waited for his lips to tug at the corners. But no smile formed. He looked so deadly serious, she wanted to run.

"It's dangerous out here."

More dangerous now, being with him. Is that why he looked so grim? Had something happened? "Why is it?"

"A call came in." The breeze tousled his hair. She remembered the texture of it at the nape of his neck. "Some guy is on the run."

"And you think he might come here?"

"With roadblocks up on the state highways, he might take a side road, try to elude everyone by hopping into someone's boat."

"I should leave then if there's—"

Standing within arm's reach of her now, with his knuckles, he brushed back the tendrils of hair flying across her cheek.

She stopped breathing, nervously tucked strands of hair behind her ear. A smile, one she'd been waiting to see, finally curved his mouth.

"I missed you." He'd made the admission with amusement, as if still coming to terms with what he was feeling. In a slow, seductive way, his fingers curled around the back of her neck and drew her face closer. "The girls are going to that sleepover tonight."

They'd be alone, wouldn't they? Her heart pumped harder suddenly.

"We could go out to dinner."

She had hunger of a different kind. As if it had a will of its own, her body swayed closer, sought the heat of his. In invitation, she raised her lips to his.

"Is that a yes?"

"Yes." She watched him lower his head, bring his lips near. "Are you going to kiss me again?"

His soft laugh answered her a second before his mouth closed over hers. She was aware of her surroundings. The scent of the lake floated on the breeze. The rustle of leaves whispered on the air. Yet all of her being centered on him, on his mouth, on the heat and firmness of those lips. And it didn't matter what had happened before or what might come later between them.

Heady with pleasure, she answered his twisting lips, met the tongue dueling with her own. The need to touch filling her, she moved her hands over his back, reveled in the heat of his body, the hardness of muscles.

Control was a breath away from leaving. Soft and pliant now, she was his for the taking. Her body tingling for more, with no shame, she clung to him, wanted to plead with him not to stop, and moaned in protest as she felt him drawing back, as his mouth began to lift from hers.

"Jess," he murmured, sounding as breathless as she felt. A hand low at her back skimmed her buttocks, and pulled her into him. She felt his hardness, the heat of him.

"Sam—Sam—"

The sound of Trudy's voice drifted through her dreamy haze.

"Damn," he muttered. Shifting, he angled away, but he kept an arm firm at her waist as if he, too, was unwilling to let the moment end, then he stretched to reach inside the cruiser and answer Trudy's message. "I'm here, Trudy."

"He's been spotted, Sam, near the Elkmans' ranch."

He took a moment before responding, "I'm on my way."

Jessica drew a ragged breath, was amazed that he sounded so composed when she felt so shaky.

"I have to leave." Lightly he framed her face with his hands, kissed her once, then again.

She wanted to hang onto him, beg him to stay, but that desperation had little to do with desire. With his words to Trudy, nerves had pulsated her stomach. Before this afternoon, she'd never considered that he would deal with anything more dangerous than someone who'd had too many beers or who had a lead foot on the gas pedal. "Is that your fugitive?"

"Might be." A hand low on her back, he steered her toward her car. "You need to leave now," he said while opening the car door for her.

Quickly Jessica slid in behind the steering wheel. She stuck the key in the ignition but didn't start it.

As he reached through the open window, and toyed with a strand of her hair, she wanted to be back in his arms. She wanted to hold him, know he was safe. Instead she touched his hand that was curled over the edge of the opened window. "You won't do any-thing—" She stopped herself, unable to say aloud words of worry. "Just don't get hurt."

Letting the strands slip through his fingers, he leaned in, kissed her once more. "I don't plan to miss tonight."

The edginess for him accompanied her drive to Casey's preschool. Though it wasn't easy, for the girls' sake, she hid her fear that afternoon. Excited about their sleepover with the Landis sisters, a four- and seven-year-old who shared their interests, Annie and Casey stuffed backpacks. Annie included a doll with a wardrobe to die for. Casey shoved her favorite rubber snake in her bag.

While they packed, Jessica wavered between pacing with concern for Sam and drawing deep breaths to combat the nerves of the first-date syndrome.

She showered, then dressed in a black designer dress with long sleeves and a scooped neckline. It was the only dress besides a long, green print that she'd packed. After brushing her hair, she slid on black pumps, then wandered into the living room where the girls were watching television.

"Jesse!" Annie's eyes rounded. "You look really pretty."

Casey scrambled to her feet, came near. "Real pretty."

Jessica felt that way with so much adoration flowing her way. "Thank you." She hoped Sam thought so, too.

Suddenly beside her, her eyes wide, Casey fingered the skirt of her dress. "It's soft."

She curled an arm around Casey's shoulder. "See

what time it is? If you're all packed, I'll drive you both to your friends' house.''

Angling a look up at her, Annie shook her head. ''Daddy would want to say good-night to us. We'll wait until Daddy comes home.''

Uncertain how late Sam might be, Jessica thought Annie might be expecting him soon. ''Annie, it might be really late.''

Not a second of hesitation passed. ''We'll wait.''

''We'll wait,'' Casey parroted.

Jessica didn't try to argue. They wore identical expressions. Mouths tightened to stubborn lines. ''Why don't I read a book?'' she suggested, to get their minds off how late it was.

''The one about the rabbit and the owl,'' Casey said and ran off to get the book.

Annie was slower to show enthusiasm. Frowning, she paused by the living room window, stared at the darkening sky.

Giving her space, she left Annie alone and sat beside Casey on the sofa. As she'd hoped, after three pages of reading Annie cuddled tight against her left side. By the time she neared the end of the book, they were spouting memorized words with her.

''And so the rabbit helped the owl build his new home,'' Annie said before Jessica could read the words.

Bending her head, she nuzzled Annie's neck. ''Yes. And so the rabbit helped the owl build his new home.''

Grinning, Annie shifted in Jessica's arms and gave

her a hug. Not to be left out, Casey fell against her. Jessica laughed and gathered them close.

"Hey, what's going on?" Sam asked from the doorway.

The girls flew at him for hugs.

"Doesn't Jesse look pretty?" Annie prodded.

"Dazzling," he said so softly, so reverently Jessica nearly blushed.

Without knowing details, she assumed he'd had a difficult day. "I'll drive them to their friends."

He set Casey back on her feet. "Good idea. While you're gone, I'll shower and dress."

"Or we don't have to go if you're tired."

He moved near, stood behind her and held the collar of her coat while she slid in first one arm, then the other. "You jest."

She felt younger. Uncertain. Tingling. Her gaze cut from him to Annie. Gently she nudged her toward the door. "I'll hurry back."

The restaurant was at the edge of town, overlooking the lake. Decorated with hanging ivy pots, brocaded booths, white linen and framed replicas of fine art, the room was dimly lit. The soft sounds of piano music played in the background.

Sam had wanted a night alone with her. It hit him while dressing earlier that they'd been chaperoned by his daughters almost every time they were together. He was beginning to feel like a sixteen-year-old whose life revolved around stolen moments, and stealing kisses.

"This is so nice," she said, surveying the room.

He wasn't interested in the view of the lake or who was there. Since they'd sat down, he hadn't been able to take his eyes off her. In the shadowy light, she was cast in a soft glow. She looked so beautiful that she'd snatched his breath away when he'd first seen her. "I like the view from here."

Spiky dark lashes raised and a smile sprang to her face. "Thank you."

He doubted she knew just how lovely she looked. Candlelight played across her face and caught the gleam of her hair and the smile in her eyes. Because he needed to touch her, he covered her hand with his own. "I've heard everything's good here."

She raised her eyes from the menu. "This isn't a favorite of yours?"

"Never been here before." He paused while water goblets were filled. "It's been a while since I've eaten out."

"Pizza doesn't count?" she teased, peering over the top of the menu at him.

As she angled a look away, soft pale skin bewitched him. "Neither does a hamburger." He dragged his gaze from her when a waiter materialized with the wine. Dutifully the man went through the ritual, waiting for Sam's approval. Until that moment Sam had forgotten how much he'd hated dating, trying to make a good impression, not mess up. He had been on dates during a brief breakup with Christina before they were married. He'd been uncomfortable with the small talk, detested having to second-guess if a movie or restaurant would please the woman.

''Did the girls say anything about us going out?'' he asked after they'd ordered.

''No, not really.'' Head bent, Jessica smoothed the salmon-colored napkin on her lap. ''Did you expect them to?''

''You never know what they'll come up with.''

''I think their matchmaking efforts are sweet.''

Sam was torn with conflicting feelings. While he agreed with her, he wasn't keen at having his daughters pick and choose the women in his life. After Christina had died, he'd never considered being like this again with a woman. He'd never wanted to be. He'd been split apart once. Gutless or not, he hadn't wanted to feel that much again for any woman. ''I guess it is. But who'd have expected matchmakers at their ages.''

''They love you so much,'' she said quietly. She was certain he knew that, but she felt she needed to tell him about what had happened earlier. ''They didn't want to leave until they knew you were home.''

A trace of sadness slipped over the sparkle in his eyes. ''They have a thing about saying good-night, especially Annie. She remembers.''

She remembers. Those two words stilled Jessica. She drew a hard breath, certain she wasn't misinterpreting what he'd said. Still she asked, ''Remembers what?''

His brows bunched as if his head suddenly hurt from a pain. ''She went to sleep before Christina came home, never said good-night to her.''

''The night...?'' He meant the night his wife had died. Jessica's breath hitched. What he'd said carried a message of so much heartache. "That's why you try to get home before they go to sleep," she said rather than asked.

"Yes, that's why."

"Dawson." At the masculine voice close behind her, Jessica rounded a look up.

A handsome couple stood beside their table. A lanky man, as tall as Sam, with a narrow face and dark brown eyes grinned with boyish charm. The petite, dark-haired woman beside him flashed a bright, friendly smile.

"So he finally took you out, Carrie?" Sam teased in the manner of an old friend as he shoved back his chair to stand.

"I twisted his arm," the woman responded.

Sam laughed, then made the introduction. "Joe and Carrie Drake. Joe owns Drake's Hardware Store in town," he added.

Jessica recalled passing it. But she needed no introduction. Through phone calls about Sam's birthday party, she'd talked to both of them.

Carrie played her part though. "We've been wanting to meet you. Joe and I are old friends of Sam."

"And getting older every day," Joe added. "You got a birthday coming up, don't you, old man?"

"Don't start." Sam turned a grin on Jessica. "He's three months younger and never lets me forget it."

"Not a minute of it." Joe's smile switched to a scowl with his look away. "Before we lose our table, we'd better go. Talk to you tomorrow, Sam."

"Nice meeting you," Carrie said before a goodbye.

"We all went to school together," Sam offered as an explanation when they were alone.

Theirs was a friendship that had lasted decades, Jessica realized. There had been Sam and Christina and Joe and Carrie. Even Liz Lewis, Sam's across-the-street neighbor, was an old school friend. And in a few moments, she'd sensed a friendship so strong that they'd have done anything for each other—anything, and expected nothing in return. "They seem so nice."

"Most people in town are."

"Your dinners, sir."

Sam leaned back and waited while the waiter set plates in front of them, then lifted his glass to Jess's. "To my good luck."

"At catching the fugitive?" Jessica raised a smile to him and clicked her glass against his.

"No." A grin softened his features. "For finding such a wonderful nanny."

Over the rim of her glass, she met the tease in his eyes. "What about the pink socks?"

Laughter crept into his voice. "What pink socks?"

Chapter Nine

Jessica had had a wonderful time. Except for those brief moments before dinner, the evening had been light-hearted and carefree. After dinner, they'd danced, then had walked along the lake. She hadn't expected such a romantic evening when he'd asked her out.

Stepping ahead of him inside the house, she unbuttoned her coat while Sam checked the messages on the answering machine. She climbed the stairs and stopped at the landing. What now? she wondered. Trying for a calmness she didn't feel, she drew several deep breaths. One caught in her throat when Sam came from the living room, then started up the stairs. "No messages?"

"None." As he reached the landing, he stepped close, narrowing the space between them.

''Guess all went well with the girls.'' She wanted to sound in control, but her pulse mocked her, racing at a quickened pace.

Featherlight, he stroked her cheek with his knuckles. ''Looks that way.''

''I had a wonderful time tonight.'' His face inches from her, she met his eyes. Passion darkened the blue, made them look fiercer. ''This was the nicest first date I've ever been on.''

Lightly his lips brushed the curve of her jaw. ''That wasn't our first date.''

As he gathered her to him, she braced for more sensation. ''That's right. We went to the ice cream parlor.''

''Nervous, Jess?''

She released a short, soft laugh. What a question. Just the sight of him made her ache. Of course, she was nervous—and longing. ''What gave you that idea?'' she asked. The will to suppress feelings had left almost the instant he'd touched her. Eyes closing, she tilted her head back to give his mouth freedom to explore her throat.

''Don't be.'' He spoke in a muffled whisper against it. ''We don't have to do anything. We won't do anything you don't want to do.''

Her pulse thudding, she thought she'd die soon if he didn't kiss her. ''What if I do want to? What if I want—'' Excitement danced inside her as his mouth lowered, sought her collarbone.

''Want what?'' he murmured against her flesh, his breath hot and stirring.

She melted into him. ''You,'' she whispered.

"Do you?" he asked hoarsely. His voice was threaded with amusement and desire. He drew back, looked at her.

Jessica met his eyes, probing hers now for refusal. Did he really believe she'd turn him down when she'd been yearning for his touch? All evening, she'd been thinking of one thing, being alone with him. It seemed as if every minute of the day centered on her wishing for what hadn't happened yet.

"I want you. I'm aching for you." He spoke on a hard breath and framed her face in his hands. "But I don't want to hurt you, Jess. If you're looking for more than the moment, if—" His voice carried a huskiness she couldn't recall before. "I don't know where this is going."

Rather than push her away, those words tugged her closer. She understood. He didn't want her to expect too much. All her life everyone had wanted something from her. How ironic, she mused. For the first time, she longed for more, and all she would have was a pleasant memory. "It doesn't have to go anywhere." She spoke words she sensed he'd want to hear.

She knew the conflict within herself, too. She didn't need another man in her life who'd pierce her heart. But the rightness she felt being with him washed over her. She didn't want to think about consequences. At this moment, her only real fear was that he would pull away again. She placed a hand on his chest, feeling his heart pounding at as quick a beat as her own. "I'm not asking for promises," she whispered.

Before he could say more, she brought her mouth to his. She started the kiss; he deepened it, twisting his lips across hers. Eyes closed, she swayed into him. She didn't want to dissect the emotions she was feeling. Desire for him clawing at her, she tightened her arms at his neck and let the pleasure of the moment sweep through her. She couldn't, didn't want to, think about anything but his taste. There wasn't room for any other thoughts, for worries about tomorrow.

Through the haze drifting over her, she was aware they were moving into his room. She heard the door close behind her. Place didn't matter—she was a creature in need of his mouth, of his hands.

She whispered his name as he lowered the zipper on her dress, as his knuckles brushed her skin, she couldn't say more. In a slow, slithering motion, the cloth flowed from her shoulders to the floor. As the coolness of the room skittered across her skin, she slid her hands under the back of his shirt and skimmed his smooth, hard flesh. He felt wonderful.

Another kiss, a few caresses—patient, sensuously slow caresses—made her feel cherished. In the moonlit room, her face inches from his, she lost herself in eyes that mirrored the emotion engulfing her. All the while, she felt a message of gentleness in the hands on her, touching her hair, grazing her body, easing down first one strap, then the other of her chemise.

Then his lips skimmed downward to the lace and heated her breast. Black lace rustled beneath his hand when he glided it down. Her skin tingled as he drew the nipple into his mouth, let his tongue circle it. He teased, he taunted, he promised to drive her mad.

Her pulse racing, she yanked at his shirt, tugged at his belt. An urgency took over. Together they tore at his clothes. She couldn't say when he moved her closer to the bed, when he lowered her to it. An impatience she'd never known before swept over her. She tasted, devoured. She touched, running her hands over his bare back, caressing hard contours, marveling at the strength of his body, the warmth of him beneath her fingers.

There was only him. With each kiss from his lips, with each stroke of his tongue licking at her flesh, with the touch of his hand seeking the dampness between her thighs, she felt the rightness of the moment, and of being with him.

Breaths mingled, lips clung and tongues dueled. Passion weaved around her, turning her skin slick. She pressed hard against his hand as an awakening blossomed within her.

When he lowered his head, when he filled himself with the taste of her, she was caught up in a mindless moment. She wanted to rest, draw breaths; she wanted him to never stop. She'd known passion before, but it had never been like this.

Growing wild, she wanted to plead. She clung to him instead. She wanted to speak words of longing, but all she could say was his name.

Spellbound, she followed the urging of his hands, moaning in response wherever his breath fell across her skin. Her breathlessness matched his. Maybe she couldn't have tomorrow, or days from now, but for tonight, she would have this memory.

No more than a moment or two passed while he

turned away to reach for protection. The instant he
leaned over her again, she strained against him, her
legs gripping at his hips. She whispered his name
once more. Heat, and the hardness of him pushed
against her. Her blood hummed. He tugged her hips
closer, murmured something soft that was lost to her,
then entered her slowly.

With a long sigh, she drew him deeper, filled herself with him until a oneness existed. When his body
ground into hers with an urgent, hard message, she
arched to meet it. All she'd imagined couldn't compare. All that she'd dreamed of with him was real.

Only the sounds of their breathing, growing more
rapid, broke the silence. Then she closed her eyes,
and all that she could give was his.

He'd never breathe normally again. Sam was certain of that. His legs caught in a jumble of sheets, he
held her to him and rolled to his back. With what
sounded like a contented sigh, she curled even closer,
nestling her head on his chest. He might be going
mad, he thought. His fingertips played across flesh
that he'd caressed and tasted every inch of. And he
still hungered for her.

Lazily she shifted. Draping a leg over one of his,
she poised above him, caressed his bare hip. "You
make me senseless," she said softly, her hand flut-
tering over to close around him.

"That's my line," he murmured as heat once more
tightened his stomach muscles. In the shadowed light,
her skin looked pale, her hair gleamed a deeper shade,
her eyes appeared brighter.

Smiling, she raised up on an elbow and sent him a look of incredulity. "Really?"

Sam kissed the tip of her nose, her cheek, a corner of her lips. "Really."

A mixture of speculation and pleasure colored her voice. "How interesting. Should I try again?" Her eyes danced before she lowered her head, kissed his shoulder, his chest, his belly.

What he planned to say hung on the tip of his tongue as she trailed hot kisses downward, as her breath heated him. He sucked in air and closed his eyes. Blood pounded in his head. His skin quivered. The ache began.

He was sure there were reasons why they didn't belong together. But with the mist of passion drifting over him again, he couldn't think of one—not now, not at this moment.

Sam awoke to sunlight streaming into the room. Even before he stretched out an arm on the bed, and searched for her, he knew he was alone. He drew a deep breath and lay quiet. He'd awakened alone for nearly two years and had never gotten used to it, but this morning he felt as lonely as he had during those first months after Chris had died. He wished Jess was still beside him. He wished they could have spent the day making love.

An unwise thing to wish for, he railed at himself and forced logical reminders forward. So far they'd played this out with remarkable honesty, not uttering false words of love. If she'd stayed, that would have added another dimension to their lovemaking. A dangerous one for both of them.

Lazily, he ran his fingers along his unshaven jaw, then slowly roused himself from the bed. His clothes were scattered around the room. He eyed the digital clock on a bedside table while he yanked on clean briefs. In minutes his daughters would return home, full of tales about their sleepover.

After tugging up his jeans, he wiggled bare feet into sneakers, then headed for the door. On the way, he pulled a sweatshirt over his head. So where did he go from here? He still didn't know why Jess had come to Thunder Lake. He believed she'd fled from someone or something. And he'd been dragging his heels to learn the truth. He hadn't wanted to press for answers. She'd claimed there was no husband. He'd have never touched her if he hadn't believed her, but why was she so secretive?

From the beginning, he'd accepted her at face value as a beautiful woman with kind eyes and a caring manner. He'd brought her into his home, he'd left his children with her, he'd made love with her. He'd trusted her. He couldn't say the same for her. He wondered what it would take to win her trust.

Stupid or not, Jessica always worried whenever everything seemed too wonderful.

Standing at the kitchen counter, she stirred the pancake batter one more time, then ladled a spoonful into the skillet. What would go wrong she couldn't help wondering? Oh, maybe nothing. Maybe she was being silly.

Earlier she hadn't felt this way. Her mood had matched the brightness of the morning sunshine when she'd awakened beside him. She'd felt warm, womanly and irresistible. He'd made her feel that way. He'd touched her with slow hands as if she were a treasure. He'd also touched her with urgent hands as if he was starving for the feel of her skin. But uncertainty danced in the air now that she stood alone in the kitchen. How would he act? Would he pretend in the light of day that nothing was different?

"I was looking for you," a voice said softly in her ear.

It was miraculous, she thought whimsically. The moment his arms slipped around her, uneasiness slithered away. "Coffee is—"

"Unimportant." He drew her back to him as if she belonged there.

Whether or not he meant for her to feel that way, she did, and all those niggling doubts she'd awakened with seemed distant suddenly.

"I need this." He turned her in his arms, kissed her once and then again, this time more deeply.

"Ah," she teased. "You believe in living on love alone." She wanted the words back the instant they left her mouth. He'd made it clear there would be no promises. "Isn't there some kind of silly saying like that?" she asked to make light of what she'd said.

His eyes smiled. "Something like that."

Jessica relaxed, grateful she hadn't ruined everything. Regardless of what she felt, she knew now what he didn't want—no love. She wished she could say the same. If this was only desire how uncomplicated everything would be, but his warning had come too late. She'd already started to fall in love with him. She wasn't certain at what moment that had happened. Almost from day one, the girls had won her heart. She'd expected that, but not this. Under different circumstances, she would have been thrilled. But where could such feelings possibly take her with him?

"You're quiet."

Unwilling to let anything snatch away this moment with him, she seized on a logical excuse for her distraction. "I was thinking about a celebration." Raising her face to him, she leaned into the arm braced against the small of her back. "It's a special day. Happy birthday." With his moan, she teasingly winked. "How shall we celebrate?"

"I have an idea."

Hanging onto the light-heartedness, she laughed. "I'll bet you do."

"We're home." Annie bounded in from the back door. "Happy birthday, Daddy."

A step behind her, Casey's voice sang. "Happy birthday."

Sam gave them his best I-don't-know-what-you're-talking-about look. "Whose birthday is it?"

"It's *your* birthday," Casey said and giggled.

Through breakfast, she and Annie kept giggling whenever they looked at each other.

Looking amused, Sam grinned when they rushed out of the room. "Guess they've got a secret. Know what it is?"

"You can't ask that on your birthday."

"Don't make any fuss. We'll go out for hamburgers tonight. The girls will like that."

"Whatever you say." For nearly a week, she'd been making preparations for Sam's birthday. The moment he left, she went into high gear. Trudy called and said she would pick up the beer and soda after work. Joe Drake arrived in the truck advertising Drake Hardware Store, and delivered the folding tables and chairs he'd collected from friends. And several guests for the evening's party arrived during the next hour, delivering various salads, Jell-O molds and desserts.

Jessica was busy cooking when Cory arrived. Minutes later, Liz came from across the street with a large lasagna casserole. While Jessica's meatballs simmered, the three women strung navy-blue-and-white streamers across the living room.

Sam's deputy, Gary Hopkins, stopped by during his lunch hour and helped set up tables and chairs for guests. The decorations were up, and Jessica was finishing the barbecue beef when the girls awoke from much-needed naps.

Trudy came after her shift that evening. Though Gary and Tony were on duty, they promised to stop in.

"That's really fancy," Trudy said about Jessica's decorating skills when she spotted the cake.

"Thank you." Jessica hadn't been filled with confidence when she'd started the job.

"Did you go to school for that?"

"I learned it from someone else." One of her family's cooks had gone to cake decorating school. At eleven, Jessica had been fascinated at the fancy desserts Lelia had made, and snuck into the kitchen as much as she could to watch her. She'd been thrilled when Lelia had let her try her hand at decorating. More than once during that summer she'd helped Lelia. That was a lot of years ago, but Jessica had gone to town, bought the necessities to do the job, and was pleased with herself that she'd remembered how to do the decorating.

"I see Joe got all the tables here," Trudy said, cutting into her thoughts. "He wasn't so responsible when he was a kid. He and Sam were a real pair back then. Nothing bad. They were just mischievous. Lately they've been quieter."

Jessica turned off the burner that was heating the meatballs. She wasn't certain how much to say about Christina to Trudy. After all, she was her aunt. "Sam's had a hard time, hasn't he?"

A soft, understanding look settled on the woman's face. "He's doing better since you came along. A lot better."

Jessica responded with a smile. She believed Sam wanted her, but the photograph of Christina was a reminder that another woman possessed his heart.

While guests arrived, Carrie Drake played lookout at the living room windows. "I can't believe we're pulling this off," she said, looking pleased.

Joining them, Joe laughed. "It'll be the first time anyone ever surprised him."

At the door, Trudy was greeting Arlene Mulvane and her daughter.

"You're looking so well," Jessica said to the woman who'd had the heart attack.

"Thanks to you." When Jessica started to shake her head, Arlene touched her shoulder. "Don't be modest. I'm just grateful you helped me." She glanced away to where Annie and Casey were standing with a few other children. "I heard from Sam that you urged the girls to make me get-well cards. That was real nice. Thank you."

"Well, they really wanted to," Jessica said, wanting to make sure she knew the girls had genuinely cared. "How are you doing?"

"Just fine now. You said your name is Jessica Scott, didn't you?"

"Uh, yes." Stress knotted Jessica's stomach. It was a usual reaction when anyone asked personal questions. "It is. Why?"

Beside her was a plain woman with hair pulled tightly back in a bun. Arlene tapped her daughter's shoulder. "When we were visiting your aunt, who did that man ask for?"

Jessica had thought her tension ridiculously paranoid. She sensed now she might have good reason for it.

"It wasn't Jessica Scott, Mother."

"Jessica something," Arlene insisted.

"Walker. Jessica Walker," her daughter answered. She sent an apologetic look Jessica's way. "Eleanor Bridgeway is my aunt. She owns a motel at the edge of town."

Jessica managed a smile and was grateful she'd stayed at a different motel when she'd first arrived in town. But who was the man? A private investigator hired by her mother or grandfather?

"He's home," someone yelled.

"Everyone dive behind something," Trudy called out.

Refusing to let the worried thoughts spoil the moment, Jessica pushed them aside. She grabbed Casey, then switched off the living room lights. With Annie on one side of her and Casey on the other, she hid, crouched down behind the living room settee.

"Smells good in here," Sam called out from the front door seconds later. "You cooked, didn't you?"

In the dark, Jessica saw Casey's bright smile. She looked as if she might bust.

"Hey, where is everyone?"

Jessica pressed her finger to Casey's lips. "Shh," she whispered in response to the little one's giggle.

"Annie, Casey. Jess—"

Lights flashed on. A chorus of, "Surprise," filled the room.

Laughter, Sam's and friends, assured Jessica she'd made the right decision to throw the party for him. She stood back, watching as he gathered his daughters in his arms, as he accepted teasing about the shocked look on his face, and she saw his smile in her direction.

While people greeted him and gave him birthday wishes, Jessica wandered to the buffet table. She set serving spoons in several bowls. Everything was on the table except the meat that was heating in the oven. With a turn to get it, she found herself face-to-face with Sam.

Without an iota of seriousness in his eyes, he delivered a pseudo glare. "Was this your doing?"

She didn't buy his act and laughed. "Do you mind?"

"You went to a lot of bother."

"Hardly any."

"Thank you." Crowding her, he brought his lips so close to her ear that the warmth of his breath caressed it. "I'll get you for this," he teased.

"Am I interrupting something?" They looked up. Steps from them, Trudy grinned. "Is he giving you a hard time?"

In an affectionate gesture, he slid an arm around Trudy's shoulder and squeezed. "Tomorrow, you pay, too. Remember all those files that need filing?"

As she groaned over his good-natured teasing, Casey danced from one foot to the other. "Daddy was surprised, wasn't he, Jesse?" she asked, throwing herself at Sam's legs.

"Yes, he was," Sam assured all of them. Grinning, he lifted Casey into his arms.

"Do I get a birthday kiss?" he asked his daughter.

"Two kisses," she answered and puckered up. "Jesse, you give him one, too."

Trudy cracked a smile. "She's got ideas."

Standing nearby, Gary guffawed.

His gaze on her, Sam actually looked as if he was thinking about it. Jessica felt her face warm.

"Sam?" Suddenly beside him, Joe smacked a hand on his shoulder. "Everyone's waiting for you to open presents."

Sam cast a puzzled look at his friend. "Since when did you become so eager for present opening?"

"Since it had to be done before I get to eat," he said, stepping away from all of them. "So come on."

"I'm coming." Laughter hung in his voice. "Jess, you come, too." He held a hand out to her. "You're a part of this."

She laced her fingers with his. For now, and for a little while longer, she was.

In the living room, the buzz of conversation and laughter overshadowed the music drifting from Sam's stereo. After inching her way down the buffet table and filling her plate, Jessica joined Annie at one of the folding tables. She was sucking on a pickle, something Jessica learned she would eat at nine in the morning if Sam let her. "You ate more than that, didn't you?"

"Yep." Her eyes smiled while she savored the pickle.

Jessica sampled Trudy's potato salad, Carrie's coleslaw, and someone else's pasta salad, then munched on a meatball. Everything tasted wonderful. She'd been raised to have more sophisticated tastes, but thought this was some of the best food she'd ever had.

"Look at Aunt Trudy," Annie said with a giggle. "She's dancing with Mr. Franklin."

The sixty-ish grocer envisioned himself as John Travolta and whirled Trudy around.

While others enjoyed their exhibition or danced, Jessica dug into more potato salad.

''Good food.'' Sam settled on the chair beside her. ''Are you responsible for that, too?''

''Only some of it. A lot of people worked hard to pull this off.''

''I need a list so I can get back at them,'' he said, smiling. ''In the meantime, I'll punish you in a different way.'' Standing, he held out a hand to her. ''Dance with me.''

She had little choice. He was already pulling her to her feet. To her surprise, he gathered her closer and pressed his lips to her jaw. She hadn't expected him to willingly link them together in any way with a roomful of friends and neighbors watching.

''You're a wonderful dancer,'' he murmured while he stroked her back. The light, loving caress was as much a seduction as his more intimate one had been.

''You are.'' At the brush of his thigh, a heat began in her belly. Lovingly she curled a hand around the back of his neck, rested her face against his cheek. An urge floated over her to close her eyes, but too many interested stares made her reconsider.

They'd barely managed one dance before shouts for the cake and a birthday song interrupted them. Good-naturedly Sam took ribbing to make a wish, then blew out the candles.

Jessica made sure everyone had something to drink. She enjoyed the praise for her cake and mentally declared the party a success.

As the evening waned, guests left. A few, like Trudy and Liz and Carrie, stayed to help with cleanup. After they left, Jessica finished washing silverware and setting up the coffeepot for breakfast.

Sam had disappeared upstairs with the girls to get them ready for bed.

Surrounded by so many wonderful people, she wished she'd come to Thunder Lake under different circumstances. She wished most of all that she'd been truthful to everyone, especially to Sam. Oh, how could she let herself fall in love with him when she hadn't been honest about who she really was? How could she not fall in love with him?

She folded the white linen kitchen towel and started up the stairs. He'd given her a precious and unexpected gift. For the first time in her life, she'd met someone who was with her not because of her money or her family name or influence, but because he really liked her.

Sam raised the blanket to just below Annie's chin, then kissed her forehead. Despite her protests that she was wide-awake and would never fall asleep, in moments she was sleeping and snoring softly.

Unlike her, he didn't feel tired, though it was past midnight. The evening had been a surprise, and while he'd never liked surprises, he'd had a good time.

He entered the hall while yanking his shirt from his pants. In his right hand, he carried his daughters' birthday presents. Annie had made a frame out of Popsicle sticks for one of hers and Casey's photographs. The present almost fit in the palm of his hand. The love it represented filled his whole body. Casey had lovingly presented him with a drawing of her fingerpainting. Seeing the giant green blob, Sam had made a guess. "A grasshopper?" he'd questioned her.

She'd beamed that he'd guessed accurately.

And Jess. All that had happened tonight was because of her. He'd been told that she'd instigated the party, contacted people, prepared most of the food. He'd learned that she'd made the cake and decorated the house. Everyone had praised her, telling him what a lucky find she was. But they had no idea what she'd really brought into his life.

Head bent, he began unbuttoning his shirt. Every moment he was with her his gut knotted with desire. And with each kiss she knocked the wind from him.

But she'd done more. Effortlessly she'd warmed a cold spot within him. She was reaching inside him. She made him want, no, need to hear her voice, to see her face first thing in the morning, and know she was near.

"Are we having a rendezvous?"

Sam stilled in midstride, looked toward her bedroom door, took in the lazy grin hiking the corners of her lips, and felt that warmth spreading through him again. "That sounds interesting."

She remained in the doorway, stood in an ethereal glow. She wore a royal blue, knee-length wrap, some kind of silky-looking thing held closed by a tie. Her face was pale, partially hidden by shadows. Sam drew in a breath and caught a hint of her flowery fragrance. It enticed him. She enticed, he reflected. Just the sight of her in that silky blue number made his palms itch. He held up his presents while closing the distance between them. "I had to get my gifts."

Beneath the darkness, her smile seemed brighter. "They were so pleased with themselves."

He wanted one more present, he realized as he stared at her face, shiny and devoid of makeup. He wanted to kiss skin that he now knew felt softer than anything else he'd ever touched. "Thanks for helping them." He bridged the distance between them. "For all of this tonight."

The moment they came together, she coiled an arm around his neck and flashed him one of those dynamite smiles that had drawn him in from day one. "I had fun."

Bending his head, he brushed lips over her collarbone. "Want to have more?"

"I can hardly wait," she murmured against his mouth. "I'm sorry. I never gave you anything for your birthday."

Those needs he'd thought about earlier blended in with wants. He released a low, throaty chuckle, amazed at how of all the women he knew this one had dazed him, made him so senseless—and so happy. Feeling the fun in her mood, he offered an assurance. "Oh, yes, you did." He recalled the time with her last night and after midnight. "One of the best gifts I've ever had."

Chapter Ten

Life was wonderful. Everything pleased her, a morning horseback ride followed by an afternoon making love before the girls came home. A day at a ranch, and then a night at the movies. For a little while, Jessica simply wanted to enjoy, not think about half-truths or deeper feelings, or about the deception she'd lived for several weeks. She didn't want to do anything that might spoil their time together.

Yesterday Sam had surprised her, coming home at lunchtime, scurrying her out the door for a picnic lunch. Like teenagers, they'd made out in the car. Last night, like a family, they'd visited Joe and Carrie.

Because of the late night, Jessica assumed the girls would sleep in. But like every other morning, she'd been up before dawn for her morning run.

Showered now and dressed in jeans and a light-weight, yellow sweatshirt, she stood by the stove making breakfast. Morning sunlight poured into the kitchen, promising a warm day. That was probably good, she thought. Sam had marked this day on the calendar that hung on the kitchen bulletin board. Below the circled number, he'd scrawled the words, Rummage Sale. She'd never been to one and was looking forward to it.

At the sound of shuffling footsteps, she looked up from the slices of bacon sizzling in a pan. Looking sleepy-eyed, and wearing his sloppiest gray sweat-pants, Sam yawned as he entered the kitchen.

Jessica flipped a slice of French toast in another pan. She expected him to grab coffee, but he slipped a hand around her, splaying his hand across her belly. "You forgot what today is, didn't you?" she said rather than asked because he wasn't dressed for anything except lazing around this morning before he left for work.

Gently he nibbled at her neck. "Whatever it is I'm supposed to be doing, I'd rather do this."

She pivoted to face him. "You won't be doing it for long," she said, hearing the clumping sound of footsteps on the staircase. In a memorizing manner, she ran her hands over the strong planes of his face. "We definitely have company." She stepped away a second before Annie dashed into the room.

Her voice sang. "I'm ready."

Ready? Sam struggled for alertness. What had he forgotten? "Ready for what?" Feeling mellow, he had to prod himself to grab the coffee cup that Jess held out to him.

"Daddy, Daddy, Daddy." Giving him her sternest look, his eldest wagged a finger in his direction.

Baffled, Sam held a palm up toward Jess, appealing for help. "What am I forgetting?"

"The town rummage sale."

An oath rose on his tongue. "Oh, da—" He cut it short, aware of his daughter's widening eyes, and quickly switched to a more G-rated curse. "Oh, dang!" For months, he'd been involved with the town council in the planning for this day. "I forgot," he said, amazed he had to make such an admission.

Jessica flipped another piece of French toast, then over her shoulder, sent him a breezy smile. "Something must have distracted you."

That was an understatement. "Something," he muttered back. In passing, he caressed her hair.

He'd planned to join Annie at the table, but she jumped up from her chair before his backside hit the seat, and grabbed his hand. "We have to go. We don't have time for breakfast. Everybody's already got all their things outside."

Jessica peered out the kitchen window to a partial view of their neighbors' lawn and that of several houses across the street. Annie was exaggerating. Besides Liz, only one other neighbor had carted out their junk already. "How much do you have to sell?"

"Not much." Standing beside the table, he gulped several swallows of coffee. "I knew I wouldn't be here. I have to patrol. And I didn't want Arlene to have to deal with too much."

Jessica assumed he'd chosen a few items so his household would be a part of the activity. "I'll finish breakfast while you're doing that."

"Want to trade?" he asked over his shoulder as Annie tugged him along.

"You always burn the French toast, Daddy."

Lovingly he stroked his daughter's head. "You always said you liked it that way."

She leveled a deadly serious look at him. "No, I didn't." Her last word flowed out on a giggle as he scooped her up.

Jessica laughed. Was there such a thing as being too content she wondered? She removed the last of the French toast from the pan, and set the batter bowl in the sink.

"Hi, Jesse."

At the sight of Casey's bright smile, she crouched down for the little one's giant hug. "Hi, yourself." Jessica thought she'd held her a little too tightly, a little too long, but Casey said nothing.

"Where's Daddy?"

"With Annie, in the garage." She noticed that instead of her usual green look, Casey had tugged on jeans and a bright orange sweatshirt. Was a new color stage beginning? "Want to get them? Breakfast is ready."

Casey didn't need to be asked twice. She darted for the door, letting it slam behind her.

In minutes they'd all be back. And she'd feel more complete, Jessica realized. She loved the three of them, loved them with every fiber of her being. There was no point in worrying about the danger to her heart. She knew now it would be broken.

"We're starving," Sam said from the doorway.

Jessica mentally shook herself from the melancholy mood that had started to slip over her. While transferring food onto a platter, she tossed a tease at him. "That was fast."

"I might make sixty thirty dollars, today, huh?" an excited Casey asked, plopping on a chair.

Annie looked up from pouring a puddle of maple syrup on her plate. "You can't make that."

Casey's little chin lifted. "Sure I can. I can make lots of money."

"Sure you can," Sam assured her in a tone meant to check their argument before it began.

Jessica wondered if he'd nurtured such calmness after becoming a father or came by it naturally. It couldn't be easy raising children alone, but from all she'd seen, he'd been successful so far.

Within half an hour they were heading outside. Excited, the girls raced ahead to the garage to cart the treasures out to the front yard.

Sam detoured to a shed and started hauling out rusty-looking garden tools. Jessica said the obvious. "Do you really expect to sell those?"

Amusement gleamed in his eyes. "Never been to a rummage sale, have you?"

What could she say but the truth? "No, I haven't."

"Here." He handed her a hoe and a rake. "Poor, sheltered thing."

There was more truth in what he said than he'd imagine.

"One man's junk is another's treasure, Jess."

And one man's ordinary life was one woman's dream come true, she admitted. Never had she imagined life like this. Almost every moment with this man and his daughters was filled with smiles, laughter and fun.

She broke every nail on her right hand scrubbing a barbecue grill clean. She stood in a fog of dust when Sam lowered an old fan to her from an overhead shelf. And she scuffed her knuckles on the brick wall while hauling the grill to the front lawn. She couldn't recall a time in her life when everything felt so right. And she didn't want to be too sensible. Just happy.

While they visited with the neighbors browsing over their junk on the front lawn, Jessica volunteered to get some cartons from the garage. Humming, she yanked a step stool close to a utility cabinet.

"What are you up to?" Sam asked suddenly.

She whipped around with a smile. "You're just the person I need."

Pleasure swept over his face. "Magic words."

"I need that carton," she said, pointing at one on the top of the utility cabinet.

Instead of reaching for it, he grabbed her hand, studied it. "You hurt yourself?"

She stared at the top of his bent head as he gently ran his fingers over the scraped knuckles. "Sam, it's really all right," she said, amused and moved by his concern.

"Is it?"

With a touch she was becoming familiar with, he gently took her face in his hands. She wished she could shout, let her voice ring out all the way to her grandfather's mansion. The man with her had done something she'd thought was impossible. He'd made her trust the feelings she felt for him and believe in the ones he felt for her. "Definitely," she murmured beneath his lips when they skimmed over hers. "And getting better every minute."

As his arms tightened, hers clung to him. A languid, relaxed sensation drifted over her. From outside, she heard Annie's yell for her sister. It was so easy to forget that they weren't alone. "We'd better get down to business," she said reluctantly.

She felt his smile against her jaw. "I'm trying to."

"We should go back. Unless you want Annie to sell your power saw for ten cents."

"She might do just that." As if he couldn't resist, he gave her a quick but hard kiss.

When he pulled back so did Jessica. She, too, caught movement at the door, and then saw Casey.

By late afternoon, most of the rummage sale items were gone. Earlier, before Sam had left, they had been like a family, the four of them standing on the front lawn in front of Sam's house, visiting with anyone who stopped, or laughing among themselves.

Now with Casey and Annie's help, Jessica hauled the things that hadn't sold toward the trash. Amazingly Sam's rusty garden tools had sold early as had the stack of mix-and-match silverware, and Annie's collection of stuffed animals.

After making sure the girls were clean and settled in front of the television, Jessica wandered into the shower. Sam had called after noon, and suggested a night at a nearby Italian restaurant. Tired, she was grateful to relinquish cooking duties to someone else.

She showered and dressed in minutes. Waiting for him, she joined the girls in the living room and settled on the sofa. They didn't look up from watching a Batman cartoon.

How different everything was now, Jessica mused. Tucking her legs beneath her, she acknowledged how different she was. She didn't need servants, designer clothes or her sports car. She'd admit that she missed the horses at home, a daily ride. She wished she could talk to her grandfather and tell him that this was what she really wanted. She wished she could make her mother understand that she wanted a different life than the one Deidre envisioned as perfect for her.

In just a few weeks, she'd become totally removed from the life she'd always known, and she was so happy. She loved baking cookies with the girls, reading to them and tucking them in bed. She loved being with Sam, sharing a walk, an ice cream cone, a quiet evening watching a video, making love. She'd found a new life, one she never wanted to leave.

"A favorite program of yours?"

Lost in thoughts, she gave a start, but smiled back at Sam. As he came closer, she affectionately punched his arm for his comment about the cartoon.

In response to his laugh, the girls' heads snapped up. Like they always did when he came home, they scrambled to their feet to rush to him for hugs.

"Can we go eat now?" Casey asked after getting her hug.

He reached down and tickled her stomach. "Is that empty?"

With a snicker, she bounced back.

Playfully he lunged toward Annie. "What about you?" Giggling, too, she skittered backwards away from his wiggling fingers.

Despite his smiles and teasing, his eyes looked tired. "Did you have a rough day?" Jessica asked with some worry.

He waited for the girls to return to their television program. Bracing his hands on the back of the sofa, he leaned over her. "A man who's floating can't get tired," he said low for her ears.

Her face angled toward him, Jessica held back a smile. "Floating?"

"All day."

"You have a silly streak, Sheriff."

"Shh, don't tell anyone." Lightly he kissed the side of her neck. "What did you do after I left?"

I missed you. How could she feel so much excitement when he was barely touching her? she wondered. "I sold all of your rusty tools."

Sam slipped out of his uniform jacket. "Knew they'd be a sure sale."

"I'm *really* hungry," Casey declared from her spot now on the carpet in front of the television.

"Well, so am I," Sam returned. Stepping back, he mouthed two words at Jessica. *For you.*

Warmth rushed her. There was nothing she'd have liked more than to step into his arms. Of course, that was an impossibility, she knew, with two sets of bright blue, innocent eyes watching them. To keep the moment lighter than she was feeling, she tapped a hand against her heart.

Casey gave another look back. "Can I have breadsticks?"

"You can have anything you want," he told her but he was looking over his shoulder at Jessica as if the words were meant for her.

You, she wanted to say. *You and your daughters.*

A crowd had gathered at Nino's, a small informal restaurant with red-and-white checkered tablecloths which was a favorite hangout. The sound of an old rock 'n' roll tune blared from a jukebox in a corner of the room. Several men and a woman razzed each other around a pool table. With Sam's hand at the small of her back, Jessica led the way to the other end of the room where a family of five chattered in a corner booth, and a couple in a nearby booth seemed more interested in each other's lips than their dinners.

"They're smooching, aren't they, Daddy?" Casey asked. "Are you going to do that with Jessica like you did this morning?"

"When?"

"In the garage. Can we play that?" she asked all in one breath and pointed at an arcade game.

"Until the pizza comes." He dug in a pocket for change and handed it to them.

Jessica kept an eye on the girls a moment longer, wanting to know exactly where they were.

"I think our secret is out," Sam said, not sounding too upset.

Jessica slitted a look at him. "If not, since Annie knows, it will be soon."

The remark brought a faint smile to his lips. "Lee?" he called out to a waitress. "Two beers." She merely smiled in response. "Beer is all right, isn't it?"

"It's fine."

"Hi, Sam," a woman said in passing.

The feminine purr belonged to a tall brunette. She wore jeans and a top one size too small to show off a knockout figure.

Tongue in cheek, Jessica smirked at him when they were alone again. "A friend?"

"I used to date her." He paused while a waitress delivered beers before them. "Years ago," he added.

Her curiosity got the best of her. "Nothing serious?"

"Teenage groping."

She could see why he'd find groping with the woman so interesting. "Was she one of many?"

"No. One of two. Christina was the other one. Once I met her, I wasn't interested in anyone else."

He looked away in the direction of the arcade games. Would she see grief in his eyes like she had the last time when he'd talked about his late wife? Was she fooling herself? She'd found something unexpected and wonderful, but what about Sam? Did he still harbor sorrow? Would he ever let her into his heart? "It was love at first sight?"

Sam lounged back in the booth seat. He wasn't

really comfortable talking to her about Chris. "I guess." He could recall memories he'd had after losing his wife, but feelings before her death were becoming dimmer. "I wanted to get married, but she was going to college, so I followed. I wasn't interested in anything then. One day on a lark, I signed up for a police science class and the rest is history."

"And Christina?"

"We married but waited to have kids. She wanted to teach."

"I thought about teaching, too," she admitted.

His gaze slid to her. "You're good with kids." Forearms on the table, he hunched forward. "Why didn't you?"

Her mother would never have approved. But it was something she'd wanted to do, a secret wish. She had no answer, could hardly disclose that she'd been expected to work on one charity or another.

"Hey, Sam, come here for a minute, will you?" a man standing by the pool table yelled, saving her from having to explain.

Grinning, Sam squeezed her hand. "Be right back."

He was well liked, Jessica mused. While weaving his way to the man, he was stopped by several people, some that were obviously friends. She had her share at home, some friends she'd known since childhood. People she should be missing, but she wasn't lonely for them.

Unexpectedly, guilt visited her again. Though she'd been away from family and friends, she hadn't felt alone since coming to Thunder Lake. Everyone had welcomed her. And while they'd accepted her into their lives, she'd been lying to them.

"I saw that hand squeeze," a voice said, breaking into her thoughts. Grinning, Liz slid into the booth.

"Oh." Jessica wasn't sure what to say.

"They're all in love with you, you know."

"I love the girls, too."

"They're *all* in love with you," she repeated, then looked past Jessica. "Sam's coming back."

"Liz, did you find someone to pick up that washing machine for you?"

She vacated the booth for him. "Cooper Raines has a truck. He said he'd pick it up for me."

Sam cocked a brow, making her laugh.

"Yes," she said to his silent question. "We're an item." Looking blissful, she slipped around Sam and toward a lanky-looking cowboy.

"How about that? Liz and the cowboy," Sam said with amusement in his voice before he settled back in the booth.

"What's so funny?"

"She's always claimed she wanted some man who'd take her away from Thunder Lake. Cooper Raines wouldn't know how to live anywhere but on a ranch."

After he learned who she really was, would he think there was too much difference between them, too?

"Daddy, Daddy," Casey gulped her words as she charged to him. "There's a carnival. Stephanie said it's here right now. Right now, Daddy. Can we go? It'll be fun. You want to go, don't you, Jesse?"

She laughed, aware how persuasive Casey could be. Seeing the smile in Sam's eyes, Jessica gave the expected answer. "I'd love to."

Casey rounded wide blue eyes at her father. "Yippee!" She dashed to her sister with her news. "We're going! We're going!"

The glitter of colored lights brightened the darkness of night. With its large midway, the carnival was sprawled over several acres of the shopping center parking lot. As they ambled close to the midway and the games, to the numerous concessions stands, the smell of popcorn wafted on the air.

Excitement oozed from the girls. Casey's small hand death-gripped Sam's. "I want to go on a black horse," she said about the merry-go-round before them.

He lifted her and Annie onto their choices, then with a hand around the pole, he leaned toward Jess and held a hand out to her. "Your turn."

Delight sparkled in her eyes. "I haven't been on one of those in years."

In a sweeping movement, Sam pulled her up and against him on the platform. He held her near for only a second, but the second was long enough for her to feel the hard beat of his heart against her breast.

"Then it was time," he murmured near her cheekbone.

"For what?"

"To have fun. And I'm long past due," he said before he lifted her onto one of the painted horses.

Jessica released a pleased laugh. Suddenly lights

glittered above like sparklers, the whirling of the ride began, the soft enchanting sound of a Strauss waltz filled the night air, and a tranquility unlike anything she'd ever felt before drifted over her.

It was a night of lights and music, amusement park rides and junk food. Excited, the girls oohed and aahed about the view of the carnival from the top of the Ferris wheel. During the ride's descent a delighted Casey screamed. Annie kept her mouth clamped tight, but her eyes flew wide, and before the ride ended, she screamed and laughed, too.

While they devoured hot dogs, they watched several locals in a corn-husking contest. Then they stopped by one of the games of chance. Sam hurled softballs at stacked bottles until he won a stuffed animal for Annie, a cuddly brown bear, and a green ant for Casey.

"That's just like the one you already have. Don't you want something else?" Sam questioned.

In a gesture of possessive affection, she placed a stranglehold on the ant's neck. "Now I've got twins."

Appearing amused, Sam shrugged a shoulder. "Guess that's important."

"Must be," Jessica said. She had no brothers or sisters, but imagined the closeness that must exist. Did sisters read each other without a word spoken, and what about twins? Was there a connection that only came to such a unique relationship?

"Hey, it's your turn." Sam curled his fingers around her forearm, jarring her to a standstill.

Unprepared, she gave him a quick grin. "What is?"

Devilment danced in his eyes when he swept an arm toward one of the other games of chance.

Jessica moaned, but good-naturedly stepped forward. Despite her best efforts, she didn't win a goldfish, but she won a blue glass dish. As the burly-looking man behind the counter handed it to her, she laughed. It would never compare with the exquisite crystal among her mother's collection, but she held it carefully like a treasure.

"You've been practicing," Sam teased. His hand at her shoulder, he aimed her in the direction of the trampoline where the girls were.

Laughter bubbled in her throat. "Right. I showed real expertise."

"We were impressed," he assured her.

"You're so easy," she said between barely moving lips as he stopped her and lightly brushed his mouth over hers.

His soft chuckle was meant for her ears only. "Glad you noticed."

While Sam kept an eye on the girls bouncing around inside the plastic bubble with the trampoline, Jessica let curiosity lead her toward the fortune teller's booth.

A woman with heavy makeup, a big-hair look and enough bracelets to weigh down her arms snagged her arm as if it were a lifeline. "You are to become a mother. This is good?" she asked.

Jessica smiled. So much for the woman's ability to foresee the future. "I'm not pregnant."

"I see what I see."

Jessica humored the woman and allowed her to run a bloodred talon down a line of her palm.

"Your lifeline is very long."

Deciding to leave while the news was good, she paid the woman and left the tent. Nearby, Sam was watching the girls slip on their shoes.

"Missed you," he said the moment she drew near. "Where were you?"

Beneath the light pressure of his hand at the small of her back, she moved with him. Ridiculously her heart had skipped a beat with his words, words that might have been nothing more than a pleasantry for the woman who'd become his lover, but she wanted to cling to them. "Learning I'm fertile."

Humor rose in his voice. "In that tent?" he asked, gesturing behind her toward the one she'd just left.

"In that tent is the Great Mystic One," she said in her best serious voice.

"Really?" Sam's grin tugged at the corners of his mouth.

"She knows all."

"Does she know you drive some man crazy?" Sam bent his head, kissed the side of her jaw, took in the flowery scent he viewed as uniquely hers.

"Do I?" she asked in a breezy tone.

Sam matched her smile. "Pleased with the thought, aren't you?"

"Ecstatic."

Chapter Eleven

"Daddy!" Her face flushed with excitement, Casey rushed to them and jumped in place. "Can I get that stuff?" she asked, pointing in the direction of a concession stand.

"Stand still," Sam insisted. Hunkered down in front of her, he looked up from tying her shoelace. "What stuff?"

"That?"

That was sticky, pink cotton candy. "And you?" Sam slanted a look at Jess.

In response, she wrinkled her nose. "I'll have an ice cream cone."

"Can I have one, too?" Annie asked.

Hero worship was settling in, Sam thought, while he made the purchases. Whatever Jess had, Annie wanted. Even though he'd seen a problem developing, he'd been ignoring it. For tonight, he didn't want to be a responsible adult. He didn't want to contemplate how his involvement with a woman he found irresistible might affect his daughters. In all honesty, he was having a devil of a time thinking about anything except his desire for her. It consumed him. Even something as simple as watching her lick the ice cream seemed erotic to him.

"Sam, you have a funny look on your face."

It's called idiocy. "I was thinking about your food choices," he said instead of admitting he was lusting for her in the middle of several hundred people. "Who'd have expected you to be a junk food eater?"

"You aren't much better." Actually, she'd had sukiyaki in Tokyo, Beef Wellington in Geneva and stuffed vine leaves in Athens, but she'd rarely had a hot dog and had never tried fry bread. "I noticed you left the vegetables when we were out to dinner."

"Cauliflower. No one likes cauliflower."

"Didn't your mother tell you to eat your vegetables?"

"Sure she did." He watched the wind toss her hair. "But not cauliflower."

From a nearby position, the girls exchanged huge grins, looking delighted to see their daddy hugging their nanny.

A palm on his chest, Jessica swayed near, offered him a lick of the ice cream. "I bet you were a cute kid."

"Adorable," he said without a smidgen of modesty. ''Done with that?'' he asked when she was finishing the cone.

Jessica tipped her head up to see his face. He looked as happy as she felt. Yes, he'd said no commitment, no promises, but she felt loved. ''Done.''

''Good.'' Sam pointed to a spot under the lights and totally visible from where they were heading. ''Girls, stay right here. And you—'' his fingers laced with Jessica's ''—come with me.''

''Where are we going?'' Her words trailed off as he drew her with him toward the twangy sounds of a regional band belting out ''Achy Breaky Heart.'' ''Sam, what are we…?'' Her laughter rippled out as he pulled her onto the wood dance floor set up by the band. Together, they fell in step with the line of dancers and matched their heel-toe steps.

Around them, laughter and shouts of ''yahoo'' accompanied the music.

Happiness filled her. Her eyes met Sam's smiling ones, shifted to the girls with their face-splitting grins. I love you all so much, she wanted to shout. ''Sheriff, you amaze me. You have many talents.''

''Glad you're noticing.''

''Oh.'' Her smile bloomed. ''I noticed before.''

As the music shifted to a slower beat, couples formed. Sam took her into his arms. ''I wish we were alone,'' he whispered against her ear.

''Me, too.'' She raised eyes to his. The moment of truth was close at hand. She had to trust him. She couldn't go on being intimate with him and not tell him who she really was. But there was so much to lose. ''Oh, Sam, me, too.''

He drew back, sent her a puzzled look. It was her own fault. There had been too much desperation in her voice. But how much she might really lose weighed heavy on her mind.

"Are you leaving, Sam?" a male voice cut in. The mayor, a short, round man, placed a meaty hand on Sam's shoulder, halting their movement. "Don't forget our meeting tomorrow."

While Sam offered a quick assurance, Jessica's private agony about her dishonesty shifted to a more public discomfort. Mentally she winced at the thought of facing the mayor and his wife again. She mustered up her best smile and delivered it to the woman beside him.

The mayor's wife returned a smile, showing a graciousness Jessica was grateful for. She obviously forgave her for the day when she'd dropped the plate of spaghetti in her lap.

"It's Jessica, isn't it?"

"Yes, it is. Nice to see you again."

"Well, actually I waved to you earlier today."

"Really?" Jessica exchanged a puzzled look with Sam. All day she'd been home because of the rummage sale.

"Yes, on the highway outside of town. I was on my way to Burns," she said about a neighboring community, "and saw you in a very fancy car."

Jessica shrugged a shoulder, not knowing what the woman was talking about. She assumed some woman resembled her. "It wasn't me, Mrs. Wilson."

Dimples cut into the woman's round face. "Then

you have a double, my dear,'' she said on a parting note.

Jessica doubted that. She exchanged a smile with Sam over the woman's words, and started to move away with him.

She had no double, but she had been leading a double life.

"Hey, Sam," another male voice called to him.

At the sound of yet another person wanting to talk to him, he swore under his breath. "I don't believe this." With a half turn in Herb's direction, Sam looked less than thrilled. "A few minutes alone with you tonight would be nice," he murmured to Jesse.

She couldn't resist a tease. "You're a very important man."

He looked definitely unimpressed with his importance. As Herb called again, he held up a hand in a halting manner. "Be right there." Reluctantly he released her. "It doesn't matter how trivial a question is. They think I should have information."

She noted the humor in his eyes. Despite his grumbling, he took his job seriously. He'd be available night and day for the people of Thunder Lake. "What was the other man's question about?"

"Fly-fishing." He chuckled softly. "Important, huh?"

She loved his smile. "Very important—to him." Glancing away, she noticed the girls busy with friends, and she spotted Cory. It had been a while since they'd talked. "While you're talking to Herb, I'll be on the bench with Cory playing catch-up."

"Okay." Though she seemed to have no problem

with all the interruptions, Sam hoped she understood. He'd never minded them before. In fact, after Christina died, he'd been grateful that people came up to him, providing him with adult conversation during an evening out. Tonight he felt annoyance ripple through him. He'd been away from Jessica and the girls all day. He wanted time with them now.

"Sorry to bother you, Sam." As if anxious to talk, Herb had met him halfway.

By the seriousness in Herb's eyes, Sam doubted he wanted to discuss something so trivial as fly-fishing. "What is it, Herb? What's your problem?"

They inched toward a shooting gallery booth and away from all the people passing by. "I don't have one." Clearly he wasn't pleased to be the messenger of whatever he had to say. "But you might. Some guy, a stranger, is asking questions," Herb said low, keeping their conversation private. "He came into the diner two mornings in a row. Said he was a private investigator. At least that's what his identification said. I remember I watched a movie about one of those private eyes, and he lied, didn't say outright who he was. But this guy did."

Sam wished he would get to the point. "What did he say?"

"Not much. The guy showed me a photo, asked if I'd seen the woman." He seemed to wait as if letting his words sink in. "He said her name was Jessica."

"Jessica?" Only a handful of Jessicas lived in town. They'd all been born and raised there. "You saw a photograph? Was it Jess?"

Herb gave a nod first. "It was, Sam."

Okay. So some guy was asking about her. "Did he say why he was looking for her?"

"No, and I didn't ask." Herb shrugged wide shoulders. "Sorry. But I told him that she had worked here."

"That's okay," he said, but none of this was okay. He should have questioned her before this, insisted on answers. But he'd been caught up in emotion for her, hadn't wanted to spoil what he'd found with her.

"You've set a date for your wedding?" Jessica asked, sharing Cory's excitement.

"June tenth." Cory's hand gripped Jessica's right one. "I was hoping you'd be a bridesmaid."

A sense of all she was going to leave behind rose within her. Friends, familiar sights, Annie, Casey, Sam. As melancholy began to grab hold, she wrestled to keep it at bay. "Oh, Cory—I'd love to." She really would. "But I might not be here."

"You won't?" Sadness entered Cory's eyes, making Jessica feel worse. "Oh, Jess, you're thinking of leaving?"

How much she didn't want to. She cared about these people. She wished she could blurt out the truth, tell her that she had another life, but this was the one she wanted, and she'd be thrilled to be her bridesmaid. "Eventually I'll have to leave," she said instead.

"Why?" Cory gave her a confused-looking smile. "Why do you have to if you don't want to?"

"Because there are other people to consider." As Cory's gaze shifted, Jessica traced her stare.

Sam stood behind her. Though he was silent, Jessica could almost hear his question. *What people?*

Standing and ready to leave, Cory touched Jessica's arm. "If you change your mind, let me know."

"I will. And thanks again," she said in parting to Cory.

Sam occupied the vacated seat. "Change your mind about what?"

"She asked me to be a bridesmaid."

Puzzlement sharpened his eyes. "You said no?"

"The wedding is in June." It physically hurt to say her next words. "I don't know if I'll be here then." She didn't try for a light mood. Too much seriousness clouded his eyes. "Did Herb have a real problem?" She spoke lightly, hoping to stir his smile, but she hadn't expected to see it. While he and Herb had been talking, she'd noticed that Herb had glanced more than once in her direction. Had Herb learned her identity? Did they both know now that she was a phony, had been lying to everyone since day one?

"No, he has no problem. We do."

Jessica stiffened. This wasn't how she wanted to tell him. Cowardly or not, for a moment longer, she dodged Sam's stare and turned her attention on the girls. Busy at an arcade game, they wouldn't be returning soon to rescue her. As silence hung in the air like a thick curtain, she made herself face him. "About what?"

"About who you are." His words came out clipped. "About why some guy is in town asking questions about you."

Panic burned her throat. She wanted to run and

hide. She wished she could magically step back in time to the first day, and have truthful words flow out of her mouth.

"This guy, a private investigator, is flashing your photo around town."

Nerves knotted a muscle at the back of her neck. She reached up, kneaded it with her fingers. *A private investigator?* She no longer had any time. Her past and present promised to collide. She supposed it was inevitable that her family would hunt her down. But she'd hoped to leave when she was ready. *And when would that be, Jessica?* she mocked herself.

"I asked you before if there's a husband or a boy-friend looking for you."

Jessica hedged for a second before she bluntly and softly blurted out, "There is a man—sort of. He wants a relationship that I don't."

"What the hell does that mean? Are you being stalked? Has he threatened you?"

She realized now that he thought fear had moti-vated her lack of truthfulness. "Oh, Sam." It was obvious that every protective instinct he possessed had kicked in. Leaning toward him, tenderly she touched his cheek, wanted to offer an assurance. "No," she said softly. "No one has hurt me. I'm not afraid."

Some of the tension tightening his features lifted. "Then what is going on?"

Jessica looked around her. She'd like more privacy when she told him. "Could we talk about this at home?" *Home. Oh, Jessica, it's not your home. You keep forgetting. That's how you really got into this*

*mess. You fell in love with two adorable little girls
and the most wonderful man in the world.*

Why she'd really stayed, why she'd kept the truth
from him had nothing to do with another man wanting
to marry her, or that her family might be looking for
her. She'd remained in Thunder Lake, clinging to this
life, because she hadn't wanted to lose the man she
really loved.

"Will we talk?" Sam questioned. "Will you trust
me enough to tell me everything?"

"I do, Sam."

Wanting contact, she placed a hand against his
chest. "I trust you more than anyone else."

"No, you don't. And I don't know why not."

She expected him to ask more, and was sure he
would have if Casey wasn't suddenly standing beside
him. As he placed a hand on her head, Jessica wondered if he'd used the contact with his daughter to
soothe himself. "Tell your sister it's time to go."

She spun around and yelled, though Annie stood
less than two feet away. "Annie, Annie, we have to
go."

Jessica moved on wooden legs toward the car. Her
heart hurt. How could she leave and give all of this
up? She couldn't leave them. They needed her.

Pressure crowding her throat, she rested her head
back on the car seat. Do they really? Her eyes smarting, she turned her face away, staring through blurry
vision at the passing scenery. They'd already endured
heartbreaking days, months, without another woman.
They'd lost Christina for good, and had survived.

Tears streaked her cheeks. *They'll manage without you. You're not that important to them.*

Caught up in her thoughts, she didn't recall the drive home. It was Sam's words that roused her. "Will you carry Casey in?"

As he cut the car engine, she nodded.

While he gathered a sleeping Annie in his arms, Jessica lifted Casey. She stirred slightly, but her eyes didn't open. It felt so natural to have her or Annie in her arms, to hold either of them.

In Casey's room, she tugged off the little one's sneakers. They'd all had so much fun at the carnival earlier. Those moments would be only memories now. She tucked them away, even the one about the fortune teller. If only the woman really could see in the future, could guarantee that this would be her family.

"Is she still asleep?" Sam asked low behind her.

"She was exhausted," she whispered. She already had Casey changed and in pajamas. "They had so much fun." *Me, too,* she yearned to say.

As if her words were unimportant, Sam leaned over his daughter and kissed her good-night.

The time had come, Jessica knew. No amount of avoidance would work anymore. "Where do you want to talk?"

Excruciatingly slow his gaze came back to her. "My office," he said in a low voice.

She didn't question his choice. As always he was thinking like a father first. His office was another bedroom at the far end of the hall. Downstairs he'd be too far from the girls, who, if overexcited and restless after the carnival, might call out to him. Feeling as if she were facing her own execution, Jessica led the way into the room. Apprehension accompanied her every step.

Sam brushed by and switched on a lamp. "Okay, tell me," he said, showing an uncharacteristic impatience.

It wasn't easy, but she met his stare with a steady one. "I'm not sure where to start, Sam."

"Start with your name. Is it Jessica Scott?"

"No, it's Walker. Jessica Walker." Beneath the dim light, she saw his deepening frown, and waited a second, gathered courage before making her announcement. "My grandfather is Stuart Walker."

"Walker? *The* Stuart Walker?" At her nod, Sam let the meaning behind those words settle in. Though Walker was a common name, it was also a prestigious one in Nevada. Stuart Walker had amassed a fortune at a young age through real estate investments and his own development company. Though the man's financial status didn't interest him, it meant that the woman before him was a heiress. He suddenly wasn't sure what to say or think, much less what to feel. Why had she let this deception go on so long? Was she having fun at his expense? Was it some whim of a beautiful and spoiled, rich woman? "Why haven't you been honest with me?"

"I never lied to you," she said in her own defense.

A coldness he hadn't felt earlier skittered across his skin. Would he have to dissect everything she said, weigh it and judge whether or not it was truth? The unpleasant notion clenched his gut. "So that makes it all right?"

"No, it doesn't." Feeling unsteady, Jessica reached back and placed a hand on the bed before she perched on the edge of it. "What can I say? I have no excuse. I needed time away from my family. I needed time to think." How silly that sounded, she thought in amazement. "Things were happening at home that made me need to get away."

"What things?" Feet from her, he braced his back against the dresser. "What made you so desperate to get away from them?"

Could anyone who hadn't lived a life filled with others' expectations understand the pressure she'd always faced? "Sam, all my life I've done exactly what they asked. I've been the dutiful daughter and granddaughter."

"What does that have to do with what you did?" Despite his brusque tone, she knew his fairness, sensed his struggle to grasp what had provoked the choice she'd made. "Were you rebelling this time? Is that what this was about?"

"No, of course not." She shook her head. "But I was tired of being intimidated."

"By them?" he asked.

She spoke an admittance softly, hating it. "Myself."

Confusion narrowed his gaze. "You're right. I don't understand."

"They didn't put nearly as much pressure on me as I did," she confessed. Somehow she had to make him understand. "I'm adopted, Sam. I never wanted anyone to regret taking me, so I've always yielded to them. But I just couldn't this time, and I wasn't sure they'd believe me if I didn't do something drastic.''

Sam had been ready to slough aside any explanation. She'd lied to him. He couldn't think of anything she would say that would excuse what she did. But nothing was ever black and white. He'd learned that early as a law enforcement officer. And while she'd talked, he'd found his anger softening. ''What did they want?''

As he sat beside her, Jessica was encouraged by his closeness. ''My grandfather is growing older. He wants an heir. He and my mother even chose a man for me—Ryan Noble.''

''They chose—'' A look of disbelief knitted a line between his brows. ''Do you like him?''

''I don't even know him.''

Sam started to smile. She supposed it was because of the ridiculousness of her story. ''Arranged marriages don't exist anymore.''

''Tell my family that.''

''You're serious.'' He inclined his head as if to see her better. ''Who is this guy?''

She latched on to the incredulity she heard in his tone, grateful for it instead of anger. ''A man with all the right qualifications. Ryan Noble is the most promising associate in my grandfather's company, and eventually my grandfather wants him to take over.''

''Did you tell them, your grandfather and—''

''Mother,'' Jessica continued.

''Did you tell them no?''

''Of course I did, Sam. I also acted like a coward,''

she admitted. "I ran from them, from the problem. But I hardly knew Ryan, so how could I marry him?" She dared a look at him. "Are you furious with me? Everything else I told you was the truth. I never intentionally lied. I know I should have told you sooner. I'm sorry."

"Why didn't you? Because you didn't trust me not to tell anyone?"

"Yes, I guess so. And I'm sorry." She couldn't say all she felt. She couldn't reveal that she hadn't told him because that would have meant she'd lose what she'd found here, that she'd have to go back to her old life when all she'd wanted to do was stay— with him.

As if reading her mind, his words offered some comfort. "Jess, you decide when you go back." The arm he slid around her shoulders gave her the most solace.

"It might be soon with a private investigator already in town."

He placed a finger beneath her chin, forced her to look up at him. "So what if he finds you? You don't have to go back if you don't want to."

"Yes, I will, or I'll have to leave."

"To go somewhere else?" A challenge colored his voice. "You can't keep running, Jess."

As if he'd poked her, her back straightened. "I'm not running." He really didn't understand. She couldn't go home yet. If she went back now, her mother would believe she'd gotten over what she no doubt viewed as "a little tantrum", and Deidre would still expect her daughter to do as she wished—marry Ryan Noble.

"What can I do to help? What do you want?" Sam asked softly.

She went with emotion, not reasoning. "You," she whispered, slipping her arms around his back. She came to the town, fleeing from all she knew, and found all she could want. She'd never forget the time with him, with Annie and Casey. She'd never forget this moment, all the moments she'd had with him.

"This isn't the answer," he said softly.

"Oh, please, Sam." She'd beg if she had to, but by the softness in his voice, she knew he wouldn't pull away. "I don't want to talk about it anymore. I don't want to think." She stilled as his hand framed her face. "Please, I just want to feel, to be with you."

Her last word died beneath his kiss. Slowly, as if she were a delicate treasure, his lips moved over hers. How could he not love her and make her feel so loved, so cherished?

As his mouth slanted across hers, a storm began to rage through her. She'd expected some of her hunger for him to have subsided. It hadn't. Like the first time, she craved him. Her mouth pressed harder against his; her tongue challenged his.

But this wasn't only about want or desire. She needed more than the physical closeness. She needed this man in her life. She needed his children to be her children. She wanted forever. And every breath drawn, every beat of her heart was for him.

She heard her name, sighed as his hand coursed down the edge of her breast, her waist, the curve of her hip. In the moonlit room, they sank to the mattress. As he pulled clothes from her, she yanked ones from him. Even before the last wisp of silk left her body, his hands were gliding over her.

Love made her ache, made her want to weep. She couldn't get enough of him. Breathless, she caressed sleek, muscular flesh. ''I want you,'' she murmured against the strong column of his neck. *I love you,* her mind cried.

She held those words to her, knowing he didn't want to hear them. A second later, no words mattered. A humming began in her head. A downpour of emotion rushed through her. With a flick of his tongue, he teased and pleasured her. As he drove her, he took her to the brink of sanity. Fire and heat dissolved gentleness. Only sensations mattered. ''Now, Sam. Please,'' she begged. Her body quivered in anticipation when she rose on her knees, when he placed hands on her hips, pulled her toward him.

Eyes met when she arched above him. As he whispered her name, she trembled. An instant later, he snatched the breath from her. He spun her world— made her senseless, and they moved together.

They moved as one.

Long after the heat ebbed, Sam kept her near. On top of him, resting, she breathed long and deep. He wanted to see her face, but for the moment was content to run a hand over her head.

Lightly, almost absently, she brushed her fingers across his chest. ''Are you tired?''

''A little.'' When she started to raise her head, he

laid his palm on the back of it, gently pushed it down. She wouldn't be with them much longer. Logic couldn't be ignored. Jessica Walker, heiress to millions, couldn't stick around Thunder Lake and play nanny for the Dawsons. "Stay," he said softly, aware this might be the last time he could say that to her.

Chapter Twelve

Strains of Beethoven's "Moonlight Sonata" wafted on the air from the piano. From the arched dining room doorway, Sam stared at Jess's slender back, watching her fingers dance across the keys. The music drifted over him, waves of sounds soaring and ebbing.

Lounging against a wall, he listened with admiration to the way she played the sequence of chords, the lulling melody. It sounded beautiful to him, artistic and refined. It was also a blaring reminder that she came from a different life.

During the past days since he'd learned the truth, how soon she would leave had never left his mind. But like ostriches sticking their heads in the sand, they'd both avoided mentioning it.

With the final notes ringing in the air, she swivelled

away from the keyboard, then smiled at him. "Have you been there long?"

"Long enough to want to applaud. Is it out of tune?"

"Not badly," she answered, crossing to him. "I never asked if you played."

Sam shook his head, welcomed the feel of her body against his.

Delicately she ran a fingertip across his lips. "Christina did then?"

"No. Her mother had. After she died, we kept the piano for sentimental reasons," he murmured beneath her fingers. "You play beautifully."

Angling her head, she smiled up at him. "Thank you. I thought you were in the garage, replacing spark plugs."

"I was but Annie's driving me nuts. So I pleaded a 'potty break.'"

She laughed as he'd hoped she would. "She's so excited about tonight's program." Ever since the girls had come home from school, Annie had been more talkative than usual.

"I know. I never thanked you for making her elephant costume."

"It was a challenge," she admitted, "but fun."

"How much longer?" Annie asked, bursting into the room.

Sam shook his head at his daughter's impatience about tonight.

"Lots of hours," he answered.

Distress bunched Annie's brows. "What if I forget

the song I'm supposed to sing?'' Behind her, Casey mirrored her sister's expression.

''You won't.'' Taking another step back from Jess, he shot a quick now-what look at her. With her shrug, he looked for a way to distract his daughter before stage fright set in. ''Come on. Let's raid the refrigerator.'' He caught her hand in his. ''Do you want strawberry or rocky road ice cream?''

''Strawberry,'' Casey yelled out behind them, determined not to be left out.

Sam took her hand, too, and headed toward the kitchen.

Jessica held onto her smile until they left the room. For three days, she'd thought of her share of excuses to avoid leaving. She'd convinced herself that she couldn't leave because Sam's deputy had to go out of town, and Sam had to work an extra shift. He needed her to stay with the girls. Yesterday, she'd used the excuse that she needed to prepare the girls for the day when she wouldn't be around anymore. But she'd let another day pass and still hadn't said anything to them. She didn't think Sam had, either. And she definitely couldn't leave today. After all, tonight was Annie's big performance in the elephant costume.

Wasn't that the best of reasons, she told herself?

Because a day would come that would steal all of this from her, she was determined to keep this one normal. After the girls had ice cream, she drove Annie to school for dress rehearsal. When she returned to the house, she started laundry, and in between, she baked some easy-to-make cinnamon rolls. With them still in the oven, Sam took over chauffeur duties and picked up Annie.

Jessica had the cinnamon rolls frosted and had just finished washing the last of three loads of clothes when Sam and Annie returned.

Filled with even more excitement, Annie pestered to have a tea party in the living room with "real" tea. Jessica poured watered-down hot chocolate into Annie's small teapot. White cups with tiny red flowers were set in place for her and Casey. The tea party included shortbread cookies, and chattering about who'd made mistakes at the dress rehearsal.

Afterwards, while the girls plopped down in front of the television set, Jessica began dinner preparations. She had the potatoes peeled and only needed to chop onions to make the meat loaf when Sam came in.

Humor hung in his voice while he washed his hands by the kitchen sink. "Is she still supercharged?" he asked about Annie.

"Yes." Jessica stepped close behind him. "And it's catchy."

Softly he groaned. "Casey, too?"

"Casey, too." Grabbing onto his light, airy tone, she slid her arms around his waist. "You know." She waited until he faced her. "You are the best onion chopper."

He chuckled. "So you want something from me."

Raising her face to him, slowly she kissed him, until he responded with a soft moan. "Absolutely." False or not, she clung to her light-hearted mood, to these moments when it seemed as if nothing could go wrong.

At the counter again, she popped a can of biscuits. Behind her, she heard Sam whistling a love song. Here was the memory she'd cling to, she reflected. Forget the moonlight, the lovemaking. It was moments beneath the brightness of daylight, like this one, that would always make her long for forever with him.

By dusk, Annie began dressing in her costume. Sam sized up the situation and decided three females didn't need him in the way.

With time to himself, he settled at the kitchen table, and while he nursed several cups of coffee, he worked on the newspaper crossword puzzle.

It wasn't hard to imagine another time, years from now, when Annie was older, just as excited, and dressing for a date. Would he be feeling just as helpless then?

Thank God, Jess was around now, helping. But she won't always be, a little voice countered. Under his breath Sam muttered a curse and shoved back his chair, annoyed by his own thought. What was the point in dwelling over what he couldn't change?

He drained the coffee in his mug, rinsed it, then headed for the stairs. This was never meant to be more than something fleeting, he reminded himself. Even before he reached the top steps, he heard Annie's and Casey's giggles. Wanting to be part of her big sister's special evening, Casey had glued herself to Annie's side the whole afternoon.

At the staircase landing, Sam spotted Jess stepping into the bathroom for a shower. "See you in a while." Looking young and flirtatious, she wiggled fingers at him, then parted her robe's opening. Giving him a come-hither look, she showed off a shapely thigh.

Sam went with her lighter mood. "Do I get to see more?"

"Later," she said in a soft, promising voice before she slowly closed the door.

"How do I look, Daddy?" a much younger voice asked behind him.

Sam swung around as Annie popped out of the room in costume. He thought she looked adorable. "You're a beautiful elephant."

"You're silly," she responded, but her blue eyes twinkled. "Elephants aren't beautiful."

"The one who lives in my house is." He ran a finger down her nose. "Are you ready?"

Instead of an expected smile, she frowned. "We can't go yet, Jesse's not ready. We can't go without her."

Sam mentally winced. So it had come to that. "Annie, you need to go early," he reminded her to get her moving. "I'll come back for her." He wavered about saying more. As much as he didn't want to force a moment of unhappiness on her, he had to prepare her and Casey. "Annie, she won't always be able to be here."

Her brows knitted with a confused expression. "Yes, she will. She likes us."

Concern for her spread through him. "Sure she

does." Sam crouched down to be at her level. "But she has a family elsewhere."

"Does she have little girls?"

He saw the tears well up in her eyes and wished he'd never started this. "No. But family. She'll have to go back to them."

Even before he finished, she began to shake her head. "No. She's supposed to stay, Daddy."

"Annie—"

She cut him off. "She's supposed to stay."

Sam matched her frown of confusion now. "What do you mean?"

Tears turned her eyes to blue ponds. "We wished for her, Daddy."

Sam had no chance to say more. With a sob, she whirled away and rushed into the bedroom. Slowly he straightened. God, how could he have let this happen?

From another room, Casey dashed out and past him. "Annie's going to be the bestest elephant," she announced to anyone who'd listen.

Rows of chairs lined the school gymnasium and were filled with family and friends minutes before the program began. Jessica led the way into one row with Casey following. In case he needed to leave quickly because of work, Sam chose an aisle seat.

Though he hadn't mentioned what Annie had said, Jessica had overheard. Inside the bathroom, stunned, she'd stood still, unable to move. With Annie's words, her heart had squeezed. Hurting the girls was the last thing she'd wanted to do.

She'd swayed against the closed door, aware she needed to leave—now—before she made the situation worse. And she needed to stop running. She needed to face her mother and grandfather, to tell them she wouldn't marry Ryan or any man except the one she loved. Until she did, she wouldn't be in control of her life.

"That was funny," Casey said, snapping her back to the moment.

Jessica stretched for a smile. "Yes, it was." She joined in the applause, though she'd missed the performance. Because nothing could be done now, she concentrated on the next acts. She even laughed during different performances, and found herself clapping enthusiastically after a piano recital.

When Annie came on the small stage with five other children and sang a song about an elephant whose ears hung low, a sense of pride washed over Jessica. That she wasn't Annie's biological mother seemed unimportant. She cherished the moment as if Annie was her own.

Applause rang in the room after the children finished. Jessica realized she'd sat in the Metropolitan Opera House and been at the opening night of dozens of Broadway plays and she'd never felt such a rush of enjoyment. Her hands stung from clapping. With the organizer's thank-you to the audience for coming, she stood to leave, as did everyone else. "It was wonderful, wasn't it?" she said to Sam when they strolled toward the exit.

Ahead of them, an excited, chattering Casey skipped alongside Annie.

"I'm not too objective," he admitted, slipping a hand beneath Jess's elbow.

Outside, a breeze blew, shuddering pine needles and rustling leaves. Jessica turned her face to the wind, letting it whip through her hair. A sliver of a moon lit the sky. She started to speak, more to herself than him. "I heard what Annie said earlier," she said, forcing the moment. She didn't look at him. Words needed to be said. "We worried so much about not hurting each other, but we forgot about them. I need to—" She paused, unable to get the one word out.

Now, in the shadowed light, their eyes met. One look spoke volumes. *Leave.* The word, unspoken, whirled around them on the wind.

"I know," Sam said softly, not needing to have her finish. "You should do it soon." It had taken more effort than he'd expected for him to say that matter-of-factly.

"You know I love them, that I never meant for that to happen."

Sam didn't doubt that she really felt that way. She'd been devoted to the girls, but what she felt didn't outweigh one fact. She didn't belong here, and neither of them could keep pretending differently. It would have been easy to draw her close, but Annie had forced this moment. He couldn't put it off any longer. "You do need to leave."

He heard her catch her breath, steeled himself against an urge to draw her into his arms. "Trudy mentioned a cousin looking for work." Not saying more as they neared the girls, he unlocked the car door, waited for them to slide in, then spoke over the top of the car to Jess. ''I'll ask her tomorrow if she wants the nanny's job.''

''Tomorrow?''

He saw more hurt in her eyes than he was prepared for, but couldn't let his own softness through. This wasn't about her—or him. This was about the girls, about not hurting them more.

Silent, she turned her face away. He didn't force conversation. Perhaps everything had already been said.

At the house, he took his time parking the car in the garage, hoping the girls would be ready for bed when he went in. Too much time with them before bedtime, and they'd read his foul mood. Soon enough they'd have to face another emotional upheaval in their lives.

And unlike the last time, this time was his fault. He should have guarded his daughters from this kind of heartache. He should have protected them.

As he'd hoped, the girls were in pajamas with teeth brushed and were waiting in bed. Sam kissed them good-night, and said nothing about Jess. Tomorrow was soon enough to sadden them.

He left the room and descended the stairs. Jessica wasn't a nanny to them. That's what he'd avoided facing. This woman who'd effortlessly worked her way into their lives had become the mommy they'd lost, the mommy they craved to have.

She's supposed to stay. He doubted he'd ever forget Annie's words. Or the tears in her eyes because Sam didn't believe that, too. *We wished for her.* Oh, damn, I'm such a lousy father, or I wouldn't have let this happen.

His heart heavy with guilt, he descended the staircase. He hit the last step as the doorbell rang.

In the kitchen, Jessica jabbed a finger at the microwave start button, and waited while her coffee heated. *Tomorrow.* Hurt rose within her. In her own mind, she'd only just set a specific date to leave. Was he in such a hurry to see her gone that he'd made plans? The heartache starting, she closed her eyes. How would she say goodbye to them?

In response to the sound of Sam's footsteps behind her, she swallowed hard before facing him. A minute ago she'd heard the doorbell. "Did someone come?"

"Guess you have no choices anymore."

Puzzled, she leaned back against the counter. What did that mean?

"They came to see you."

"Me?" Now she was more puzzled. She had a few acquaintances in town, but no one who'd drop in so late. "Who is it?"

"He said his name is Ryan Noble."

Ryan? How? How could he have known where she was? Who'd told him? Who could have? A sick sensation settled in her stomach. Only Sam. He'd have had to do it before she announced plans to go home. No wonder he had someone in mind for her job. He knew she'd be leaving. "You called my family? Why did you call them?"

His eyes snapped in her direction. "Why did I *what?*"

Believing the worst, she couldn't quell her temper. "Why did you call them?"

Disbelief flashed across his face for only a second. "I didn't call them," he said slowly as if measuring out the words to her.

"Then how…?" She stopped, grabbed a calming moment to stifle her own anger. "How did they know where I was?"

"Back up." Even though his voice remained quiet, his eyes heated with emotion. "You really don't have any idea what trust is, do you?"

So many people had played her for the fool, had had ulterior motives for being with her. She'd truly believed that Sam had none. But then why would he? She'd been a woman who'd appeared down on her luck, needing a job. He hadn't known her real identity. But once he learned she was a Walker, he hadn't wasted much time contacting her family. What he would gain didn't really matter. She really didn't want to know what he'd get for betraying her trust. "You want me to go. Is that why you called them? Or did my grandfather promise you something for telling them where I was?"

He shook his head. "I don't know you." As if muddled, he shook his head. "But then you don't know me if you'd believe that."

"I guess not." Jessica didn't stall. Not waiting to hear what else he might say, she rushed past him in the doorway, and headed for the foyer.

Tall, raven-haired, Ryan gave her a bright smile. Jessica couldn't return it. Her heart was breaking. All this time while she'd been falling in love, Sam had never felt more than desire for her. She'd known he didn't love her, but she'd really believed that he'd cared about her. But if he had truly cared, he wouldn't have betrayed her like this.

Feet from Ryan, her stride faltered when peripherally she caught movement to her right. As a woman stepped out of the shadows, Jessica's heart stopped. In less time than it took to draw a breath, her world tilted. Across the room, her mirror image stared back at her. The woman, who had the same auburn-colored hair and stood the same height, stared at Jessica with blue eyes so much like her own she couldn't look away from them.

A second passed, then two. On unsteady legs, Jessica moved forward, labored to breathe, to speak. "Who—who are you?" she demanded as an eerie chill raced up her back.

A smile that matched her own curled the edges of the woman's lips. "I'm Sarah—Sarah Daniels. I know this will be a shock, but—" She paused, drew a deep breath. "There's no other way to say this. I've learned we're twins."

"Twins?"

"Yes," she answered softly.

Denial came on the next breath. She had no family. She was adopted. Who was this woman? While she moved closer to the woman and Ryan, from the corner of her eye, she saw Sam turn away from the doorway.

She ached to call him back, wishing he would stay. She needed someone on her side, someone beside her. Of course, he wouldn't stay. He wouldn't want to after what she'd said to him. And she shouldn't want him after he'd betrayed her, but emotion couldn't be switched off with the quickness of snapping fingers. Unsteady, she sought support and perched on the arm of the sofa. How could she have a twin she never knew about? "I don't understand."

"I don't really have all the answers," the woman named Sarah said, settling with Ryan on a settee opposite her.

Jessica couldn't take her eyes off her. Just what was the connection between them? Could they really be twins—sisters? "How did you learn about me?"

"Ryan—" Sarah grew quiet as he, in an affectionate, a loverlike way, slid his hand over hers. "Ryan came looking for you, and we met. It was then I realized that I had a twin."

A twin. This was real. She had a sister, someone of her blood, someone she was connected to. "You never knew before this?"

"No, I didn't," Sarah answered. After Ryan came into my life, we went to Willow Springs, saw Stuart, my—our—grandfather," she said and smiled. "It seems strange to say that. I've never had a grandfather before this. When we talked to Deidre, she told us how worried she was about you. She asked us to find you."

"And you came here after you got a call from the sheriff?"

Sarah frowned. "A call?" She slanted a look at Ryan. "No, that's not how we found you. The private investigator your mother hired notified her that he might have found you."

Jessica shut her eyes for a moment. She'd forgotten about the private investigator who was nosing around town.

A deeper frown settled on Sarah's face with her next words. "Ryan said you had left because of him."

In an appealing gesture, Ryan hunched forward. "No one should have tried to force you into anything, Jessica. I apologize for that. Sarah made me see how wrong this was. But—" His face split into a wide grin. "I do have to thank you. Because of you, because you fled to avoid marriage, I took off to find you. I found Sarah instead." Love and adoration warmed his eyes as he looked at Sarah. Briefly he explained that he had barged into Sarah's life as she was about to marry another man, thinking she was Jessica. "I'm not here to force you into marriage. I'm here to tell you that you can go home and not worry about that." His arm slid around Sarah's shoulder. "We're engaged."

Nothing he could have said would have surprised her more. "You're—you're engaged?" How strange this all had turned out, Jessica mused. "So you came here because of a call from the private investigator?"

"Not exactly," Ryan answered. "We called your mother, and she told us that the private investigator learned a woman named Jessica had worked in a local diner several weeks ago. It seemed unlikely you'd be doing that, but we decided to come here anyway and check it out."

Sam, what have I done? He'd said she didn't trust him. He was right. She'd judged him so unfairly, expected the worst from him. He hadn't called anyone, she knew now. And he hadn't betrayed her. Oh, why hadn't she trusted him? Why had she acted so foolish? She knew Ryan was talking, but her mind was with another man. Why would she be so distrustful of a man who'd shown her only kindness and caring?

Because people had used her. Repeatedly in her life she'd been taught the same lesson. At eight years old, she was the first one chosen for the free-style swimming team at the country club, though several other girls were far better. She was the first choice, not because she was the best, but because she could provide an Olympic-sized pool in her backyard for practice. In her teens, boyfriends were never hard to find once they learned who she was, and how influential her family was.

But no one had ever broken her heart until Nathan. She'd loved and believed in him, and in one afternoon, during one meeting with her mother, he'd proven that his love for her money mattered most.

The lesson learned had been painful, one she'd never forgotten. In her world, love, even friendship, often came with conditions.

"Deidre's really concerned about you," Ryan said.

Jessica forced herself back to the conversation at hand. Before this, she'd thought her mother only wanted to find her to force the marriage on her. But Ryan and Sarah were engaged. Deidre must have known that when she sent them to find her.

"She thought you might be angry at her," Ryan added.

Jessica had been. She'd believed that her happiness

hadn't mattered to her mother, but now she wondered if she'd been too hard on her.

As if trying to see what wasn't visible, Sarah studied her. "It's so strange to look at someone who looks exactly like yourself."

Jessica had been thinking the same thing. Were they linked in ways beyond their appearance? "I don't understand any of this. What do you know about us, Sarah?"

"According to Deidre, she never knew you had a twin."

Jessica wondered if that was true. Though never malicious, her mother often twisted truth to suit herself. "Where were you all this time?"

"I was raised in Bellville, Nevada."

"So close," Jessica said softly.

"It is strange, isn't it?" Sarah agreed. "I was told that I was ill when I was born and placed in foster care for the first five years. Eventually I was adopted. The people I view as my parents, Edward and Alice Daniels are gone now, but they were wonderful to me."

Jessica was happy for her, but she couldn't help feeling some guilt. She'd led such a privileged lifestyle, and though Sarah didn't complain about her life, clearly she'd had a difficult time during the first five years.

"I need to get answers," Sarah said in a determined tone.

Jessica nodded agreeably. "About our birth mother."

Sarah's brows bunched with her frown. "Yes. I

didn't have the money to investigate, to find out more. But you could have. Why didn't you before this?''

The challenge didn't surprise Jessica. Sarah Daniels came across as quiet but independent. She would have never let important questions about her adoption remain unasked. ''I didn't want to upset my mother. The one time I tried to discuss it with her, she became upset,'' Jessica told her. At eleven, she'd been sensitive to everything. Tears in her mother's eyes had devastated her.

''What do you know?'' Sarah questioned.

Jessica brought herself back from her thoughts. ''I know she was a Las Vegas dancer. Our father had an affair with her.'' Jessica explained that Deidre was married to him, and after his death, learning about the woman and her pregnancy, she went to her to adopt his child.

''But you don't know her name?''

''No, I don't. I told you,'' Jessica said in her defense, ''My family—my grandfather and mother, didn't like to talk about the adoption, about my— our—father's unfaithfulness. It seemed such a painful time for my mother that I didn't ask her too many questions.''

''I can't be so delicate,'' Sarah said. ''I want answers from Deidre. I want to know our mother's name. I want to know why she kept us apart, why she let Deidre believe there was only one baby.''

''Yes, we need to get answers.'' They were long overdue, Jessica realized. But as difficult as that confrontation with her mother might be, far more painful for her would be leaving the girls and Sam. Now that her past had caught up with her, her life with Sam was crumbling anyway. Having accused him of something he hadn't done, she wasn't even sure he'd talk to her. Sadness filling her about him, she told Sarah she'd go pack.

She hadn't counted on finding the girls waiting for her in her bedroom.

"Why do you have to leave? Did Daddy make you mad?" Hammering out questions, Annie clung to her side when Jessica went to the closet. "Did we make you mad? We'll be good."

Sitting cross-legged on the bed, Casey piped in with her assurance. "Uh-huh. Real good," she said with an emphatic nod of her head.

Annie went on, "We don't want you to go. Please, Jesse, don't go."

Their tears flowed.

Emotion swirling through her, Jessica sat on the bed beside Casey and opened her arms to both girls. Her heart ached for them, for Sam, for herself. Most of all, for all they might have had together.

While Annie leaned into her, Casey climbed onto her lap.

"We thought *you'd* stay."

The words weren't said but Jessica heard the hidden message in them. *Our mommy didn't.*

"Please, please, please, Jesse." Annie's eyes begged. "Please don't go."

Against her neck, Casey sniffed.

I'm sorry. I'm so sorry. Unable to speak, Jessica simply hugged them. She kissed Casey's tear-streaked cheek, caressed Annie's hair, wished with all her heart for what they wanted, wished she could stay.

Cuddling the girls, she looked up, saw Sam standing in the doorway. *Tell me you love me.* If only he'd say those words.

"You could come back," Annie said, shifting the direction of her wishful pleas as if guessing the failure in begging Jessica to stay.

She looked for something to comfort them. "I'll always be with you."

Eyes shining with tears, Casey looked up at her. "How can you be if you're not here?"

If nothing else, she had to be truthful with them. "Because you'll always be in my heart."

"That's not the same," Casey wailed.

No, it wouldn't be. She wouldn't have the feel of their arms around her in a bear hug, wouldn't know their kiss on her cheek or hear an excited story about their day. She scanned the small faces. Tears swam in Casey's eyes. Annie nibbled on her bottom lip, barely holding back a sob.

From the corner of her eye, Jessica saw Sarah standing in the doorway. She waited, then cleared her throat before asking softly, "Are you ready to leave?"

Never, Jessica thought. "I'll call both of you." Jessica squeezed each of them, then forced herself to pull away. If she lingered, she'd make this moment more painful.

As she started to draw back, Casey clutched at her. "Please, Jesse, don't go."

Oh, God. Jessica blinked against the smarting behind her eyes. Drawing a tremulous breath, she clung to both of them. When you love someone, you don't hurt them. Hadn't she been looking for that kind of love all her life? Knowing that, how could she do what others had done to her; slip into their lives, hurt them and leave?

Raising her head, she caught movement, and noticed Sam moving away from the doorway, coming closer. "Casey, come on," he said when near.

At her father's touch on her shoulder, she turned away, let herself be lifted into his arms, then buried her face in his neck.

Gently Jessica caressed the top of Annie's head before releasing her hold on the little one. Annie cried openly now and threw herself against her father.

Jessica made herself stay for another moment. She could have rushed from the room, but Sam deserved her apology. Nervously she shifted her stance as his gaze fixed on her face. "I'm sorry, Sam. I'm so sorry." If only he loved her. *If only.* "I was wrong about you." She swallowed the tightness in her throat. "Unfair."

"Jess—"

"Please don't be angry," she interrupted.

"I'm not," he said softly.

She wanted to cry. She wished he would yell at her. Maybe he really did want to, but with the girls in his arms, he was controlling emotion, stifling his anger. Maybe he would never forgive her for hurting all of them so badly.

"You've had a shock," he said then with all the

willingness to understand that he'd shown her from day one.

How like him, she realized. As angry and disappointed as he must have been with her after her accusation, instead of words about himself, about what she'd said to him, he was thinking about what she was feeling. "Yes, learning about Sarah was a shock. But that doesn't excuse what I did earlier. I've learned you didn't call them. I should have known you wouldn't. I could give you excuses, but—"

He shook his head, quieting her. "You don't need to."

Hurt sliced through her. How could he be so indifferent, unless she really wasn't important to him? She had to fight herself to not reach out and beg. "I'll send someone to get my things," she said abruptly and turned away.

At the door, she paused. She wanted to look back and didn't dare. She kept walking, with the sound of Casey's and Annie's sobs echoing in her ears.

Sam hadn't given Jess a lot of time to talk—he couldn't. When he'd taken Jessica's place on the bed and had held his daughters, he'd felt their bodies tremble with sobs.

With some difficulty, he stared at the two sweet faces before him now. Sadness, the kind they'd all endured before, was wrapping around them. It was so much like grief that his chest physically hurt. Wasn't this what he'd wanted to avoid?

"What did you do to her?" The accusation strengthened Casey's voice.

"She couldn't stay," Sam said, figuring that was the only answer they needed.

Annie pulled back, fixed watery blue eyes on him. "Like Mommy couldn't?"

He hated their tears. He was never certain how to handle them. "No. This is different. Your mommy wanted to stay and couldn't."

Those weren't the right words, Sam knew instantly.

Annie's voice broke. "Didn't Jesse want to?"

He brushed a knuckle across her cheek. "I don't know." He felt so inept. Don't look at me for answers, he wanted to say.

Annie's body shook as she sniffed back tears. "Daddy, you could make her stay."

He couldn't make her stay, not even for them. Once before Annie had begged him for something, and he'd failed. It seemed like yesterday when he'd sat with them in the hospital waiting room, when they'd waited for the doctor, when Annie had pleaded with him.

"Mommy will be all right, won't she?" she'd kept asking.

Nothing had been all right after that.

Both a plea and hope filled Annie's voice. "Please, Daddy, you could get her back."

How sure of him she was. Didn't she remember he'd failed them once before? He hadn't been able to bring their mommy back. And he couldn't make everything right this time either.

Chapter Thirteen

It was strange. Because she'd changed, Jessica had expected everything she'd left behind to be different but nothing was.

She entered her grandfather's house, a formal red brick two-story. The mansion in Willow Springs looked as lovely as ever with its circular driveway and manicured lawn and flower gardens, but she wished she was in a much smaller house in Thunder Lake. Standing in the elegant foyer, she watched her mother's approach and prepared for the next difficult moments.

A petite woman with blond hair, lovely for her years, Deidre spent hours at the salon and spa to maintain the look. "What were you thinking, taking off in the middle of the night, leaving us a note that you'll call?'' she asked in a sharp tone that had always worked well at making Jessica acquiesce to whatever she wanted.

"I wrote more than that, Mother."

"Oh, yes. I have no difficulty recalling your silly words."

It occurred to Jessica that her mother still didn't understand that she needed to live her own life.

"Discussing your actions is unimportant now. You're back and plans need to be made. You've heard about Ryan and Sarah." She cast them a polite but not terribly warm glance. Jessica read her mother well. She was not happy that Ryan had chosen Sarah. "Since they left to find you, I hired a private investigator to look for your birth mother."

"What?" Sarah whirled around. Surprise registered on her face. "Why didn't you tell us before we left that you planned to do that?"

Deidre stiffened her back. Who did this girl think she was to make demands?

"So you did know our mother's name?" Sarah asked, a hint of an accusation in her voice.

Deliberately Deidre shifted her stance. She'd mastered the art of putting others in their places. Unless the girl was stupid, she'd feel that she'd been subtly shunned. Ignoring her, Deidre crossed to Jessica. Her daughter would be less critical of her when she made her announcement. "Yes, I do know. Larissa Summers was the woman's name."

"Was?" Jessica asked.

"I'm sorry that I don't have better news." Because it would convey more sympathy, she pivoted toward

Sarah and Ryan to include them in her conversation. "The private investigator discovered that Larissa died in an alcohol-related car accident."

Deidre looked away. What a mess she'd nearly made of everything. She had never wanted to bloody her hands to keep the secret from Jessica and now the other one—Sarah. Fortunately all would be all right now. She'd felt enormous relief when she'd learned the Summers woman was dead, that she wouldn't have to resort to such desperate measures as having the woman killed. Luck had been with her.

"What else did the private investigator learn?"

"Nothing," she offered as a response, not wanting to share more. Unlike the man she'd had searching for Jessica, "private investigator" was hardly an accurate job description for the burly man with greasy hair who'd been looking for Larissa Summers. He was a professional assassin, he'd told her rather proudly. It had required more courage than she'd expected to contact him, to offer someone money to kill another. But she'd had little choice. She couldn't let anyone talk to Larissa Summers. To her amazement, he hadn't had to do a thing. Larissa was dead, by the hand of some drunken driver. Regardless, Deidre knew her secret was safe. Jessica wouldn't learn the truth.

No one knew the truth except her and a midwife, and no one would find the midwife. The secret would remain just that. Even her lawyer didn't know, Deidre thought rather smugly. When he'd handled the birth certificate for Jessica, he'd only been aware of twins, Jessica and the baby Larissa had kept. No one had known there was a third baby, that Larissa had given birth to triplets.

Feeling calmer from her own thoughts, Deidre strolled to the window, stared out at the perfectly landscaped lawn. Behind her, Jessica and her sister talked in hushed tones. How close they'd become in such a short time.

They should never have known about each other. Fate played cruel games, she decided. Were they so close now because she'd taken both of them from Larissa? At the time, she'd thought the old man would love having his son's twins. She'd been willing to endure another woman's brats to be in Stuart's favor. After Lawrence had died, she'd have done anything to make Stuart happy, to stay in the family fold. She'd needed a link between herself and the Walkers. If that meant being mother to her late husband's bastards, so be it. She would do whatever it took to keep herself close to the Walker fortune.

But then one baby had seemed ill. She didn't need a sickly brat. She eyed Sarah over her shoulder. She hardly looked ill anymore. Rather than take her home with her, Deidre had left Sarah at the closest hospital. Would Stuart forgive her if he learned that? No, neither Stuart nor Jessica, with her sensitive heart, would understand her abandoning a baby.

She must stay calm. With Larissa gone, neither Stuart, Jessica nor Sarah would ever learn what she'd done, or that another sister existed. There was no reason for them to even look or ever realize that Larissa had kept a child, that her only daughter was the missing triplet. And California, where she lived, was a world away.

"Jessica." Stuart's booming voice caught all of their attention.

Jessica smiled with her grandfather's approach. She'd missed him, she realized in that moment. Turning from Sarah, she rushed to him for a hug.

"Don't you leave us like that again," he reprimanded. A tall man with silver hair and aristocratic features, he was quite handsome despite being in his seventies. "I was worried sick about you."

"I'm sorry, Granddad," she said, returning his hug.

Drawing back, he stared for a long moment at her, then winked. "You, too," he called out to Sarah. "Come here."

Smiling, she crossed to him and slipped into the space offered by his arm outstretched to her.

"I can't believe my luck. Two beautiful granddaughters. Aren't they beautiful, Deidre?"

"Yes." A stiffness hung in her mother's voice. "They're beautiful."

Someone who didn't know her mother well might have believed her smile. Jessica knew better.

"Soon we'll have a wedding." Joy rushed into Stuart's face. "And Ryan will be family after all."

Ryan returned his smile. "I'm happy to say that I will."

For the first time in months, Jessica felt no pressure to marry him hanging over her head. She should have been relaxed and happy. But her heart was heavy, her thoughts elsewhere.

"Sweetheart," her grandfather said to her now,

"all I ever wanted was what was best for the family. I never meant for you to be so unhappy."

"It's all right, Granddad." She presented the smile she sensed he needed to see. Everyone was smiling except her mother. Deidre wore a tight semblance of one. With his words, it occurred to Jessica that her mother, not her grandfather, had been pushing for the wedding.

While he talked to Ryan about his wedding to Sarah, Jessica stepped away from the foursome. Her father's photograph sat on a nearby Queen Anne table. Had her mother loved Lawrence Walker? Or had everything been about the Walker fortune? How desperate she must feel all the time. Was that why Deidre had been so frustrated, so angry when she'd refused to marry Ryan? Had her mother feared that the child she'd raised would do something wrong and fall out of favor? Perhaps everything was about the money.

"You must be tired," Sarah said suddenly behind her.

Jessica returned her smile. She felt exhausted, weary of smiling. "You, too. Come with me. I'll show you to your rooms. The east wing?" she said in a questioning tone to her mother.

"Yes, that will be fine."

Linking her arm with Jessica's, Sarah paused her on a step. "You've been really quiet. Why don't you call the girls?"

Jessica touched her hand. "I guess I'm pretty obvious. I'm sorry if I'm lowering your spirits. This is such a wonderful time for you and Ryan."

"You don't have to apologize to us for missing all

of them,'' Sarah said as they reached the top of the staircase. ''I'd be the same way if I was away from Ryan.''

Grinning at her words, Ryan slid an arm around Sarah's waist. ''What are you going to do about it, Jessica?''

She mustered up a soft laugh. He sounded so positive she would. ''There is nothing to do.'' She showed them to their rooms, sure they'd use the connecting door, then went into her room.

The huge room with its rosewood furniture and canopy bed had been her haven all her life. Tonight it was just another room in the house. She thought about another home, another bedroom. Sitting on the bed, she remembered her promise to Annie and Casey. She'd promised to call. As painful as the next few moments would be, she geared up for the sound of Sam's voice and punched out his phone number.

Instead of Sam's deep voice, a feminine one answered.

''Trudy?''

A silent second passed. ''Jess, is that you?''

''Yes.'' Jessica felt badly about deceiving a woman who'd offered friendship from the first day they'd met. ''Oh, Trudy, I'm sorry that I wasn't truthful with you from the beginning.''

''Don't worry so. Sam explained.''

Explained what? Jessica wondered.

''He said that you had your reasons. Good reasons.''

Did that mean he really had forgiven her for everything? Regardless, she said a silent thank-you to him. She would hate to think that people she considered friends would have viewed her as a liar because she'd given them a false identity.

"Sam's not here right now," Trudy said even though Jessica hadn't asked for him.

"I called to talk to the girls."

"Oh!" Jessica heard the frown in Trudy's voice. "Sure, I'll get them for you, but—listen. Jess, I have to say what's on my mind. They need you. He needs you. You're the best thing that's happened to them."

"Trudy, thank you, but—" Without any warning, a tightness rose in her throat. She wished all of that was true. I miss all of you, she wanted to say.

"I mean that. I guess you can't come back, but I wish you could. You all seemed so happy together that I'd hoped—well, I guess it wasn't to be."

For the next fifteen minutes she talked to the girls, but the conversation was difficult. They pleaded and cried for her to come back. Before she said goodbye, she decided this would be the last time she would call them. There was no point in keeping in touch. She might even hurt them more if she didn't end this.

Her spirits didn't improve over the next two days. Fighting melancholy, she was tempted to stay in bed. That wasn't her choice, she knew. Though time had passed since returning home, since that last phone call with the girls, since the last time she'd seen them and Sam, her heart seemed to hurt more. She missed them. She missed the three of them so much that she thought she'd die from the loneliness for them.

Easing out of bed, she berated herself. There was

no point in a pity party. It wouldn't resolve anything or lessen the emptiness she felt.

Quickly she dressed, then left the room. As she descended the stairs she prepared for the day ahead. Recently her mother had been talking about social obligations. The last thing she wanted to do was plaster a smile on her face and pretend her life was wonderful.

Nearing the bottom step, she heard her mother's agitated voice. "This won't do."

Jessica reached the dining room to see that a rush of color was brightening her mother's cheeks.

"I expect fresh strawberries every morning," Deidre was complaining to Rawlings, the Walkers' long-time butler.

"Who's making all the noise?" At the doorway, his hand linked with Sarah's, Ryan grinned in a way that made Jessica assume he already knew the answer to his question.

"It's a household problem," Deidre said with a backward wave of her hand. "It's no concern of yours."

"What's no concern of his?" Jessica's grandfather questioned, suddenly appearing at the arched doorway.

"Everything is all right," Deidre snapped in a voice meant to end all the questions.

While Jessica joined her mother at the buffet table, Ryan and Sarah wandered toward her grandfather at the dining room table.

Disgust oozed from Deidre's voice. "Do you see?

None of it is fresh,'' she said, lifting the lid of a silver dish to reveal a bowl of fruit compote.

With a plate of food, Jessica ambled to the table to join the others. It didn't matter to her if the fruit was fresh or whether Deidre would chair a charity or if the stock exchange plummeted. She wanted to know if Annie passed her math test, if the bully in Casey's preschool class was still giving her a hard time, or if Sam had taken time for lunch yesterday.

Her heart and mind were in Thunder Lake. At this time in the morning, she'd be pouring cereal in bowls for the girls, and while they ate, she'd be making sandwiches for lunch. She'd be seeing the girls' smiles and feeling Sam's arms around her.

''A bird eats more, Jessica,'' her grandfather said from his seat at the head of the table as she set down her plate. Looking content, he dived his fork into a mound of scrambled eggs.

Jessica responded to him with a smile. She loved her grandfather dearly, but she felt out-of-step with him and her mother. While he resumed discussing business with Ryan, she abandoned the idea of eating. *I don't belong here anymore,* she realized. *I really don't.*

In need of air, she wandered to the terrace door and stepped outside. She'd never be the same person. She'd changed. With Sam, she'd been her own person, made her own decisions. No one had told her what to do or expected anything from her. No one had tried to make decisions for her.

Overhead, heavy pewter clouds blocked the sun, threatening a drizzle. Was it raining in Thunder Lake?

She remembered a television weather report the morning she'd left. The meteorologist had announced an incoming cold front accompanied by a rainstorm. Was Annie using her new purple umbrella?

"Tell me what's wrong?"

Jessica jumped and whipped around, startled by her grandfather's voice behind her. As his strong hands cupped her shoulders, she surrendered to the ache within her. "Oh, Granddad." Tears flowed and words about Sam and Annie and Casey spilled out of her.

Showing wisdom, he listened but offered no advice.

Jessica was grateful. There was nothing either of them could do to change everything. Only Sam could.

At her grandfather's urging, she reentered the house with him. Though she had no appetite, she ate the croissant and fruit on her plate, but she wanted to be alone.

Rain hammered at the kitchen windows. Sam figured the weather matched his dismal mood. Standing at the kitchen sink, he sipped his morning coffee. In the distance, he heard the rumble of thunder. He rubbed at his forehead trying to ease the dull thudding ache he'd awakened with.

Hearing the girls running down the stairs, he pivoted away from the window and readied himself for his daughters' bright smiles. Yesterday they'd moped, but kids were resilient, and he expected some kind of excitement about the day ahead.

He was wrong.

Casey came in with a long face. Trailing behind

her, Annie looked as if she'd lost her favorite doll. No, it was worse. They'd lost the woman who'd found a place in their hearts.

"Can I call Jesse?" Annie asked instead of saying good morning and plopped down on a chair at the kitchen table.

Casey shuffled in to join her. "Do you have her phone number?"

His back to them, Sam poured cereal into two bowls. "I don't have the phone number." That was the truth, though he knew he could get it. He placed the bowls before them, saw Casey nudge her sister with her elbow. What conspiracy existed?

"We want to call her, Daddy." Annie set down her spoon and abandoned the chocolate-flavored cereal. "Something could be wrong. She said she'd call and she hasn't."

He sensed breakfast wouldn't go well this morning. "She did call you," Sam reminded them. He'd been surprised when Trudy had told him about her phone call, but also grateful. "Two days ago."

"That's a long time," Annie told him.

An eternity, Sam reflected. It seemed like forever since Jess had been with them.

Casey's chin clung to her chest. "Why do people go away and not come back?" A tremor weaved into her voice, indicating that she was a breath away from bursting into tears. Slowly she raised wet, glassy-looking eyes at him. "Jesse won't come back, will she?"

Sam's chest tightened. If she cried, he was a goner.

"Doesn't Jesse love us?"

His heart turned over at the sight of tears streaking her pudgy cheeks. "Honey, she loves you. Both of you." He believed that or wouldn't have said it to them.

As Casey bowed her head and let tears flow, Annie patted her back to console her, but her own bottom lip trembled.

"Come on, girls," Sam cajoled, crouching before them and seeing the misery on their faces. A sick sensation lumped in the center of his stomach. "I know you miss her."

Watery blue eyes stared at him.

"We love her, Daddy," Annie said on a sniff.

Dammit, how could he have let this happen?

How could he have stopped it? he realized.

He couldn't keep them from opening their hearts to her. Such courage, Sam mused. They knew it hurt to love and lose someone. And still they took that chance.

He hadn't been as brave. He hadn't wanted to go through the heartache of loving and losing again. He hadn't wanted to feel again. He didn't want to miss someone so badly that it ached to breathe whenever he thought about her. So he let her go, because he hadn't wanted to hurt again.

Yet here he was—hurting.

Mentally he cursed. He was such a fool. He'd believed if he didn't make a commitment to Jess, then he wouldn't feel too much. But words weren't needed. She already had his heart.

"Daddy?"

He looked up. Hopeful faces stared hard at him.

They see right through me. They know I could get them what they want. This time the only thing preventing that was his lack of guts. They all could have Jess in their lives if he'd stop acting like a coward.

Deidre stalled by the buffet table, staring at her daughter's slender back. Jessica hadn't moved away from the terrace doors. What was wrong with her? She was no longer required to marry Ryan. Yet, she'd been acting so odd since she'd returned home. Deidre shuddered slightly as she recalled the report she'd received about her daughter from the private investigator. What had possessed her to perform the duties of a servant, especially a nanny to someone's snot-nosed brats? "What are you mooning about?" she asked in a low voice.

Jessica faced her with a wounded look.

Too sensitive. She was much too soft.

"He'd have wanted something from you, Jessica," she said about the sheriff that her daughter had had some little fling with. "They all do."

"You're wrong, Mother. He didn't want anything from me."

Deidre watched her turn away. So naive. So ungrateful. All she'd ever asked of her daughter was to present the right image as Stuart's heir. Annoyance grabbing hold again, she darted a look at the woman who resembled Jessica. They were nothing alike. And what about the third one? What was she like? What did it matter?

Deidre drew several deep breaths to calm herself, to stay in control. Somehow she'd prevent the three sisters from ever meeting. Enough of her plans had already been spoiled.

She cursed the situation, allowed her fury only a few seconds to bubble within her. If Ryan hadn't met Sarah Daniels, the plan to see Jessica married to him would have eventually worked.

Now self-preservation made her offer Sarah her best smile. This one didn't know her place. However, like it or not, she was part of the family now. Disagreeable as it was, Deidre knew she would have to get close to her dead husband's other illegitimate brat.

"I'll have coffee, Rawlings," she said to the butler. She would continue to do anything to remain on Stuart's good side. Slowly she stirred the sugar in her coffee. If only Jessica had done what was expected. If she'd stayed put, none of this would have happened.

Ryan Noble, Stuart's next in command, should have been her son-in-law. He was the connection Deidre needed to remain on Stuart's favorable side. If all had gone as she'd planned, after their marriage, Ryan would have provided Jessica with a child. That child, her grandchild, would have been Stuart's great-grandchild and would have guaranteed secure futures for all of them.

Now she would have to rethink her plans.

Chapter Fourteen

Jessica had felt as if she'd suffocate in the house. She excused herself, murmuring an explanation about needing to go for her morning jog. Thankfully no one, not even her mother, had protested her leaving.

Her mother would never comprehend what she'd found with Sam. To Deidre, love came with conditions. All her life Jessica had believed that. Because she was adopted, she'd always felt as if she had to do what was expected of her to keep her mother's love. Annie and Casey had taught her differently. All they'd ever wanted was her love and affection.

Though it was nearly midmorning, she changed into sneakers and took off across the back lawn into the woods at the back of the house. She followed a dirt path, running harder than usual, needing the wind tossing her hair, looking for some distraction to free her from her thoughts about Sam and the girls.

Earlier she'd played a game, trying to convince herself that the void in her heart would disappear. Instead it seemed even more intense.

Today was Friday, "share day" for Casey at pre-school. Jessica wondered if she'd taken her rubber snake to school. Had Annie learned a new story? Did they miss her as much as she missed them?

Oh, Sam. Sneakered feet hit the dirt path harder. Never had she wanted to see anyone so much. He was such a brave man, a tough, ex city cop. He'd weathered his share of dangerous moments. Why hadn't he let himself take another chance on love?

As the house came into view, drifting clouds shadowed the morning sunlight. Jessica spotted Sarah coming out the door. Lost in her own misery, only then did Jessica remember a promise to go horseback riding with Sarah.

Learning where the Walker mansion was had taken no work at all. After his frowning daughters had trudged into the living room to watch television, Sam had called Trudy and told her to get Gary to take his shift, and that he'd be gone at least one day, maybe more. He'd scooted the girls into his car, waiting until he'd driven to the halfway point before he'd made his announcement that he was taking them to see Jess. Their excitement filled the car during the hours of traveling and escalated when they passed through the security gates of the Walker estate.

"Does Jesse really live here?" Annie sounded as

full of disbelief as he'd felt while he'd waited for clearance from a security guard.

As they made their way up the winding drive that led to the mansion, Sam glanced in his rearview mirror at his daughters. They were both gaping. Sam knew Jess had money, but he wasn't prepared for the house and the grounds with the swimming pool, tennis court and stable. He slowed his sports utility vehicle to take in everything, and spotted Ryan Noble standing beside a sports car in the driveway.

"She has horses. Daddy, she has horses," Annie said excitedly, practically jumping in her seat despite the seat belt strapped across her.

"Are they Jesse's horses?" Casey asked with more restraint, displaying her usual show-me-before-I'll-believe-it attitude.

"I don't know. They might be her grandfather's." Sam braked behind the sports car. As he switched off the ignition, Ryan approached him. "Stay inside," Sam told the girls before he climbed out of his vehicle.

Though they'd only recently met, Sam relaxed slightly when he saw Ryan. He'd looked besotted whenever he'd stared at Sarah. Sam figured if anyone knew how he was feeling, that person was Ryan. "The girls were worried because they hadn't heard from Jess in days," Sam said when Ryan met him halfway.

Ryan craned his neck to look past him at the girls. "So they made you come?" Amusement danced in his eyes. "I thought you might have come because you wised up."

He could have told Ryan that it wasn't easy to face feelings honestly. "Is she home?"

Instead of answering, he said, "You know, she told Sarah and me something during the drive here. She had good reasons for hiding out, Sam. She told Sarah that all her life she wasn't accepted for herself. People saw her as Stuart Walker's granddaughter, heiress to the Walker fortune. I think she really enjoyed being with people who didn't know that."

Sam had gotten the same impression. He didn't tell Ryan that her deception wasn't what had sent her away from him. His stupidity had.

"There was a man, Nathan something, who'd hurt her. She was young, seventeen, really loved him, but her mother considered him all wrong for her. As if to prove she was right, her mother offered him a hearty check if he'd leave Jessica alone. He proved what mattered more to him, took the check, and left without a word to Jessica. She learned about this from her mother after she waited four hours for him to show up for a date."

Sam hadn't met Jess's mother, and would reserve judgment until he did, but someone with more sensitivity wouldn't have put her through such humiliation.

"Jessica told Sarah there had always been someone who wanted something from her." Ryan shrugged a shoulder, looked guilty. "I wasn't any better. I hardly knew her but was going to marry her because of the Walker money, the company. In the end, it all worked out. I found Sarah and fell in love."

As he looked past him, Sam swung around and saw

Jessica and Sarah leading their horses back toward the stable.

"I hope Jessica has, too," Ryan said.

Head bent, Jessica watched her feet, kicked at the dirt with the toes of her boots. She and Sarah had discussed their mother throughout the ride. It was so hard to understand what had made her give up her babies.

"We need to go to Promise," Sarah said about the town where Larissa Summers had supposedly lived.

Walking beside Sarah, Jessica transferred the horse's reins to her other hand.

"Unless you have something else to do," Sarah said.

She could have told her sister that there was nothing to stop her. She had no commitments, no one waiting for her return. "No, I'm free to go. What about you? Will you be staying here with Ryan now or returning to Bellville?"

"I gave up my job at the bank. Since Ryan has the business to be concerned about, we'll make our home here in Willow Springs probably."

Regardless of where Sarah was, Jessica knew that a closeness that had begun days ago between them would strengthen. She had a sister now, a best friend unlike any other.

Sarah brought the horse, a palomino, close and patted its nose. "Someone should know something about Larissa."

Jessica squinted against the glare of the sun. It seemed so wrong to feel nothing for the woman who'd given them life. When Deidre had said Larissa was dead, Jessica had felt no sorrow, though disappointment had swept through her. She would have liked to meet the woman, talk to her, learn what her thoughts and her situation had been that she'd given up her twin daughters. Having been with Annie and Casey, she couldn't comprehend how any woman could give up a child willingly.

"When do you want to leave?"

"Soon." Jessica made a request. "Sarah, don't say anything in front of my mother about our plans to go to Promise. I don't want to hurt her feelings."

"I'm surprised you feel that way." Sarah tipped her head questioningly. "You're not very close, are you?"

Jessica saw no reason not to be truthful. "Not really. I think my mother always feared falling out of favor with my grandfather. Since she never had children, when my father died, she had no link to Grandfather or the Walker money. I believe that's why she really adopted me." Saying that aloud hurt, but Jessica couldn't deny what seemed true. "It was her way of producing a Walker heir, of remaining a part of the family." After she'd said the words, she realized how cold and calculating that had sounded.

"You really believe that?"

Jessica knew the truth wasn't flattering to Deidre, but she wanted her relationship with her sister to be based on truthfulness. "Yes, I do," she admitted. "I think it's also why she pushed for my marriage to Ryan who was my grandfather's fair-haired boy. I love her.'' She met Sarah's stare squarely. ''I really do. But I don't always like her.''

Sarah reached out and touched her arm, but anything else that might have been said remained silent as youthful voices danced in the air.

Frowning, Jessica turned in the direction of the sounds. At the sight of Casey and Annie, Jessica's heart jumped. ''Oh, my gosh,'' she cried out. She took off running to meet them. One moment nothing had been right, and now nothing was wrong.

Dying to hold them, she dropped to her knees and opened her arms to them. With exuberance, they threw themselves at her, nearly knocking her over. How was this possible? What did it matter? On a laugh, she enveloped them in her embrace. It didn't matter why they were here. She was holding them. Nothing else was important. What she wanted and needed was here.

''We missed you,'' Annie said.

''I missed both of you.''

Jessica looked up despite Casey's death-grip hug on her neck. That's when she saw Sam. Why had they come? What did he want?

''Annie, Casey.'' Sarah stepped forward and extended a hand toward them. ''Want to see the tree with the birdhouse in it?''

As if afraid to leave Jessica's arms, they didn't budge.

''It's all right,'' Jessica assured them.

Casey's eyes were wide, like before, as she looked from Jessica to Sarah, then back to her.

"Go ahead," Sam urged his daughters. "I need some time alone with Jesse."

Looking hesitant, Casey stood firm for a long second, then ran to Sam. "Daddy." She grabbed his hand and tugged on it so he'd bend over. As she whispered something to him, he lovingly ran a hand over her head. "Go with Sarah," he urged, touching her back.

Jessica wasn't certain what was happening, but she mouthed a thank-you to Sarah for taking the girls away so she and Sam could have a private talk. Nerves close to the surface, she steadied herself with a long breath. "Why are you here?" Seconds ticked by. Sunlight beat at her back. The fragrance of daisies drifted over her. But her world narrowed to the space that separated them.

"The girls missed you."

She pressed her lips firmly together. She'd truly hoped he would say something else. Was that why they'd come? Had the girls badgered him until he gave in? With effort, she veiled her disappointment. "I missed them."

"I could see that. The girls wanted to see you." Sam damned his own verbal clumsiness, but was having a tough time telling her what a fool he'd been. "Tell her we love her. Tell her we want her to come home" Casey had said.

What if she said no? What if…? Even as his own vulnerability rocked him, he took a step closer. "Oh, hell, Jess. That's not what this is about." She'd left because he hadn't offered her a choice, and he'd yet to say anything to change that. "I've been thinking."

Brilliant, Dawson. "That's all I've been doing for days. Thinking—and missing you."

"Missing me?"

"Yes, missing you." She deserved everything from him, even a little groveling. "When Ryan came, I took the easy way out, pushed you away. I though it would protect the girls. Protect me," he admitted. "I really believed that if I didn't love, I couldn't get hurt."

Her eyes softened. "Oh, Sam."

He couldn't deny what he felt, not any longer. Love. He loved her, and he was still keeping the words inside. "I love you, Jess. I think I fell in love with you the day you stuck your finger in my water glass. But I didn't want to admit that even to myself.

"I've been holding back. I figured I had it all once. No way would I get another chance. I hadn't even been sure I wanted one, wanted someone else to lose." He touched her upper arms, said a silent thanks that she wasn't pulling away. "The girls never doubted you. They believed you were supposed to stay. That's what they told me. Only I was too stupid to see that."

"I'd have stayed if you'd asked," she said simply. As she slowly closed the distance until only inches separated them, Sam struggled not to crush her against him. "But I thought you might not want to see me anymore, couldn't forgive me," she said with such pain in her eyes.

"For what?"

"For hurting all of you."

He leaned his head forward and pressed his forehead to hers. "I'm the one who hurt us," he made himself admit. "All I had to do was tell you that I loved you, and I could have prevented all of this."

He hadn't said nearly enough, but she placed her fingertips on his lips as if to silence him. "Oh, Sam, I love you, too," she said softly.

With a shake of his head, he released a quick, short laugh, amazed at how stupid he'd been. "Jess." For a moment he couldn't say more as tension flowed from him. "I was only existing until you came along. You make me smile, make me feel whole again." He met eyes filled with love—for him. "If I tell you that I want to marry you because I can't live without you, will you say yes?"

Jessica let out a sigh. "That's all I ever wanted to hear." She made a small sound as he slipped his arms around her. Tears of joy blurred her vision. She'd never known how little she really had until she'd met him and the girls.

"We're a package deal, you know."

Jessica heard giggles, looked to her left and saw Annie and Casey's wonderful smiles.

"Will you marry us?"

"I'd love to marry all of you," she said on a soft laugh, raising her lips to his.

"Jessica?"

At her grandfather's voice behind her, she dragged her gaze from Sam. In a studying manner, her grandfather's eyes narrowed. "Do we know each other?"

She kept an arm firm on Sam's back. Please like this man, she wanted to beg her grandfather.

Sam held out a hand to him. "Sam Dawson."

"Of course." With no hesitation, he shook Sam's

hand. But his smiling blue eyes focused on Casey and Annie. "Are these the little ones you told me about, Jessica?" Not waiting for a response, he went on, "They're prettier than you said."

While Annie beamed, Casey giggled.

With a few, warm words, he welcomed them. Until that moment, Jessica hadn't realized how important that was to her.

"What in the world is going on?" Deidre's voice carried an edginess that suddenly made the moment less bright. Jessica would have offered an introduction but her mother's gaze shifted from Sam to the girls, and she said the obvious. "You're the sheriff with the daughters?"

"That's me," Sam said with an ease that conveyed a desire for friendliness. No one intimidated Sam Dawson, Jessica had been told by more than one person in Thunder Lake.

"Why are you here?" Instead of friendliness, Deidre's voice carried a haughty tone that made Jessica cringe.

Tension crackled in the air. Jessica felt it. So did Sam. *Be nice to these people,* Jessica wanted to yell at her mother. *I love them.*

As if echoing her thought, Sam answered. "We're here because we love your daughter."

Jessica's eyes filled with tears. How wonderful those words sounded.

A beaming Sarah sidled close to Ryan. "I think a double wedding would be perfect," she announced out of the blue.

Jessica watched her grandfather's eyes widen with surprise, her mother's jaw sag, and Sam's smile slowly form. As Sarah's eyes sparkled with good humor, Jessica guessed her sister had deliberately chosen a way to startle everyone.

"Is that all right with you, Sis?" she asked without any awkwardness.

Jessica smiled back at her, felt the bond between them tightening. "I'd love it."

In unison, both Annie and Casey yelled with joy.

Standing to Jessica's right, her mother winced at what Jessica assumed she viewed as noise.

"Can we be in the wedding, Jesse?" Annie asked.

"We couldn't have one without you two." Jessica laced her fingers now with Sam's. "Would that be okay with you?"

"What are you talking about?" Deidre asked before Sam could respond.

Jessica hoped to avoid a scene. "I'm getting married, Mother."

Nearby Sarah grabbed Ryan's hand. "Let's go to the stable. Would you girls like to see the horses up close?"

They looked hesitant. Jessica sensed they wanted to hang around, make sure all went well.

"Go with her," Sam urged, seeming as alert as Sarah had been that Deidre might voice objections and upset the girls.

"Wait." Deidre demanded everyone's attention. "I want to know about the wedding you've planned."

Because of the girls, Jessica preferred no confrontation now. "We haven't really planned anything yet, Mother. Except that it will be a double wedding."

"A double wedding." As if some thought was taking form, Deidre's eyes blanked. Then suddenly and unexpectedly her voice softened with a speculative tone. "I think that might be quite wonderful."

Though pleased her mother wasn't critical of the plan, Jessica felt a touch leery. Anytime her mother agreed easily, she prepared for a second shoe to drop.

Enthusiasm rose in Deidre's voice. "Everyone who is anyone will want an invitation. This will be *the* event of the social season."

Now she understood. If her mother had control of the wedding, the Walker mansion would present the most spectacular one of the new millennium. Jessica angled a glance at Sarah. She simply rolled her eyes, not looking thrilled at the idea of too much hullabaloo.

But showing wisdom, Sarah didn't argue, and set a hand on each girl's shoulder. "We'll go see those horses now."

"A theme wedding might be nice," Deidre said, already discussing her ideas.

Jessica's grandfather looked amused. "It's their wedding, Deidre." Jessica saw the twinkle in her grandfather's eyes before he caught her mother's elbow and propelled her toward the house. "Leave the planning to them."

Watching them, Jessica said a thank-you for his interference. As always, her grandfather would be the one to keep her mother in line.

"Finally, we're alone," Sam said, drawing her attention back to him. "Think your grandfather approves?"

Her head reeling from all that had just happened, she coiled an arm around his neck, and flattened herself against him. "He knows I love you."

"Does he?"

"Yes. You gave me something I never had before. For the first time in my life I was cared about for myself. My grandfather realized all that when we were talking earlier."

His eyes became serious. "Ryan mentioned something like that to me."

Jessica recalled how much she and Sarah had shared of their lives during the drive from Thunder Lake to Willow Springs, and how often Sarah and Ryan had smiled or laughed at the same thing. "I'm so glad he and Sarah found each other."

"I'm glad we found each other." His hand pressed against her back as if to assure her that he'd never let her go. "I love you more than anyone else ever will." He seemed to pause, draw back slightly, then his eyes swept over the grounds of the estate. "But you have to know that you have more than I could ever give you."

"No," she said with love filling her. She draped an arm over his shoulder, and regarded the girls racing back from the stable. "You have more than I ever expected to get." Joy bubbled within her as the girls dashed to her and Sam. She caught Casey while he lifted Annie into his arms.

"Kiss her, Daddy," Annie insisted.

"Gladly," he murmured, and skimmed his mouth over hers.

When he deepened the kiss, Jessica smiled beneath it, then closed her eyes. All the wealth in the world couldn't equal the treasures she'd inherited today.

* * * * *

*Turn the page for a sneak preview
of next month's*

HERE COMES THE BRIDES *title,*

*the compelling conclusion to this
Silhouette Special Edition continuity—*

EXPECTANT BRIDE-TO-BE

by Nikki Benjamin.

Chapter One

Jack followed Abby into her mother's small, wood-frame bungalow, trying not to feel too embarrassed by his neediness. He had fully intended to see that she got home safely, then be on his way. But by the time they got to the modest neighborhood where she'd grown up, he could hardly bear the thought of spending the rest of the evening alone.

Being with Abby had brightened his spirits enormously. In fact, he couldn't remember enjoying a woman's company so much since he'd been on his own. Odd, because Abby wasn't anything at all like Cindy. She was smart and funny in her own special way—a way that appealed to him even more than he'd originally anticipated.

Taking Abby out to dinner hadn't turned out to be

quite as casual an affair as he'd intended—at least not for him. Her presence across the table had filled him with a warm glow of contentment. Selfishly, perhaps, he'd wanted to hang on to that long forgotten feeling.

He'd coerced her into offering him a drink before he could think better of it, and had been so relieved when she agreed. Just a quick drink, then, he'd go. Or so Jack had told himself until the moment she took him by the hand and led him into the house.

The first flicker of an altogether different, not to mention far more intimate, yearning sizzled along his nerve endings, while low down in his belly, another kind of warmth began to uncurl. And no matter how insistently he told himself to ignore it, he was intrigued by the possibility that suddenly came to mind.

He should leave *now*. He should, but hell if he could—

"Is something wrong?" Abby asked, looking up at him with a slight frown. She had stepped into the tiny entryway, still holding his hand, while he stood, as if rooted to the spot, on the threshold.

"No, not at all," Jack assured her, making a valiant effort to pull himself together as he joined her.

"You don't have to stay if you've thought of something you need to do instead," she added, letting go of his hand.

He had, but not in the way she meant. And though she'd given him an easy way out that he should gratefully take, he wasn't going to do it. He had resigned himself to living what had become a very lonely life. He hadn't realized just how much he'd missed the feelings now coursing through him—the comfort of companionship laced with the heat of desire, the wanting and needing, ignored for so long, that had reared up when he was least expecting it.

"No, there's nothing." He looped an arm loosely around her shoulders, a first foray into territory he was suddenly, unashamedly desperate to explore.

Abby seemed a bit startled by his gesture, but she didn't pull away.

"Well, then, let me take your jacket."

The entryway of the little house opened directly into the living room. With the flick of the light switch on the wall, Abby lit the lamps on a pair of glass and brass end tables framing an old sofa upholstered in a faded rose and green floral print. The multi-colored lights on the Christmas tree, standing in the far corner, lit up, as well, adding a poignant warmth to the room. An easy chair and ottoman, covered in a green and beige pin-striped fabric, a brass and glass coffee table and matching etagere filled with an assortment of books, porcelain figurines and framed photographs completed the furnishings.

Though Jack was accustomed to more elegant surroundings, he was immediately drawn to the coziness of the room. Here was a place where two people could sit together, close enough to touch, and talk about anything their hearts desired.

"This is nice," he said, reaching back with his free hand to close the front door.

"Thanks," Abby murmured as she stepped free of his hold.

Before he could offer his assistance, she slipped out of her coat and hung it on the old-fashioned, carved oak coat tree that stood off to one side. Then she turned back to him, a quizzical look on her face.

"What?" he asked, not quite sure what was expected of him.

"Your jacket." She smiled slightly. "Unless you've decided not to stay, after all."

"I'm staying." He returned her smile sheepishly as he shrugged out of his jacket and hung it up himself.

He'd been so caught up by the way she'd moved around the entryway—coming so near to him in the close quarters, yet not quite touching—that he'd been able to think of nothing but pulling her into his arms, pushing her up against the wall, kissing her senseless and...more than likely, scaring her half to death. Cursing silently, he gave himself a firm mental shake.

USA Today Bestselling Author

SHARON SALA

has won readers' hearts with thrilling tales
of romantic suspense. Now Silhouette Books
is proud to present five passionate stories from
this beloved author.

Available in August 2000:
ALWAYS A LADY
A beauty queen whose dreams have been dashed in a
tragic twist of fate seeks shelter for her wounded spirit
in the arms of a rough-edged cowboy....

Available in September 2000:
GENTLE PERSUASION
A brooding detective risks everything to protect the
woman he once let walk away from him....

Available in October 2000:
SARA'S ANGEL
A woman on the run searches desperately for a reclusive
Native American secret agent—the only man who can save
her from the danger that stalks her!

Available in November 2000:
HONOR'S PROMISE
A struggling waitress discovers she is really a rich heiress—
and must enter a powerful new world of wealth and
privilege on the arm of a handsome stranger....

Available in December 2000:
KING'S RANSOM
A lone woman returns home to the ranch where she was
raised, and discovers danger—as well as the man she once
loved with all her heart....

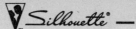